T0367821

The
Watch

MICHELE KNECHT

ARCHWAY
PUBLISHING

Archway Publishing books may be ordered through booksellers or by contacting:

Archway Publishing
1663 Liberty Drive
Bloomington, IN 47403
www.archwaypublishing.com
1 (888) 242-5904

ISBN: 978-1-4808-8141-9 (sc)
ISBN: 978-1-4808-8142-6 (e)

Library of Congress Control Number: 2019911780

Print information available on the last page.

Archway Publishing rev. date: 9/30/2019

This book is dedicated to my beautiful parents in heaven, who unknowingly left me their watches before they passed and inspired me to finish my book. I miss you every day.

ACKNOWLEDGMENTS

To my husband, Todd, and my daughters, Brandie and Lisa, thank you for supporting me through this project. I love you with all my heart. To my sister Theresa, for selflessly listening night after night, page after page. I would never have been able to get this done without you. To my sister Cathy for reading my book and supporting me throughout. To my sister Gloria, for suffering chapter after chapter, line after line editing my project. I couldn't have completed this without you. To my sisters Esther, Rita, and Mary for always believing in me. To my brothers, Paul, John, Pat, and Mike, you need to read my book! I have the greatest family in the world. I love you all.

CHAPTER 1

Katie

Have you ever tried to do something in your life only to find out you were railroaded into something else because of fate? For Katie's entire life, she had thought that things happened to other people that way, but not to her.

Katie was working at a local pizza shop in town when the man of her dreams walked into the restaurant. She was sure she had seen him before. Maybe she had seen him on TV.

Katie thought she knew what she wanted out of life. She thought she knew where she was going, and that no one would stop her from attaining her dreams or her goals. That year, she would be graduating. She was in the twelfth grade and knew she was headed to college in the fall. She had dated a few boys during her high school years, but she had never gotten serious with any of them. This guy took her by surprise. He was gorgeous, though not like the other guys she was attracted to. Usually, her taste in men ran to the typical tall, dark, and handsome. This guy was short and blond, and something inside her went pitter-patter when he spoke to her.

Even with the man of her dreams so close, work was work, and the restroom needed cleaning. Katie headed toward the back of the restaurant with a mop and bucket in tow. The man came up behind her and asked if he could wheel the bucket for her. She said, "Sure!" She took the mop, and he took the bucket. She turned to thank him as she approached the back of the restaurant, but he was gone.

After Katie finished cleaning the restroom, she asked her boss if she had seen the guy who'd helped her wheel the mop bucket. The boss said she hadn't seen anyone come into the restaurant. Katie was disappointed, but she knew she would see him again—maybe not that day or the next, but she would see him again.

After work that night, and from that day on, Katie found herself obsessively wondering about the mysterious stranger who had walked into her life that night at work. She couldn't say why, but she couldn't shake off thinking about him. *Who was he? What was his name? Where was he from?* So many questions, but there were just a few more months before graduation now. She decided the craziness about her mystery man had to stop.

Katie already had so much on her plate. Graduation would be here before she knew it, and there were plenty of projects and papers to finish before then. She had been working a lot at the restaurant too, but was looking forward to leaving that behind to start an internship at the hospital next month. In three more months, she would be off for the summer. If she could hold on until then, some of the pressure would let up.

One day, after work, Katie took a walk near the old

cemetery. Something shiny on the ground caught her eye, and she bent down to pick it up. It was a watch—and it looked like an expensive watch at that. She turned it over and saw initials engraved on the back - KO. How curious. They were her initials. KO- Katie O'Reilly. Her heart started racing, and her mind was going in a million different directions. She thought, *Who does this watch belong to? Who has the same initials I do? Where did it come from?* She had to get some answers, and her nana might just be the person to have them.

Katie had started living with her nana after her father passed away and her mother, who wasn't able to deal with his death, was institutionalized. Since she knew Nana was going out for the evening, Katie ran home as fast as she could. Perhaps Nana would know something about the watch, but Katie would need to hurry to catch her before she left. Unfortunately, Nana's car was gone. Katie wouldn't be able to find out anything until morning.

The next morning, Katie woke up and sat next to the window before she went down for breakfast. For some reason, it was harder to get out of bed that morning. She said her morning prayers and thought about the watch she had found the night before. *Who on earth would have lost such an expensive watch in this town?* She knew the Sampsons, the wealthiest people in town. No one had those initials in that family. The other wealthy people from that simple town were the doctors. She knew most of them, and again, none had those initials. She headed to the kitchen to see if Nana could think of anyone with those initials—other than Katie, of course.

Nana had just finished breakfast and was reading her Bible when Katie walked in with the watch. The kitchen was small, and the cupboards, built by her papa, were unique. The patterns he had put into the woodwork were extravagant. Katie's papa always had said nothing was too good for Nana. Papa had passed away two years before. He had been popular with people in town. Everyone who had known Edward O'Reilly had liked him and respected him.

"Nana, can I ask you something?" she said with a quiver in her voice.

Nana looked up over her reading glasses. "Yes, dear?"

"I was wondering if you could tell me who in this town has the initials KO."

She looked at me questioningly. "Is this a trick question?"

"No. I know I do, Nana, but is there anyone else who has those initials?" she asked with a little more conviction.

Tears ran down Nana's cheeks. "Well, Kat, your grandfather's real name was Kevin. He used the name Edward because he had an uncle he lost as a boy whom he loved dearly, and he wanted to take his name to honor him." She smiled, clearly thinking about Papa. "What's on your mind, Kat?"

"Well, when I went for an afternoon walk, I found this watch near the old cemetery. It looks like an expensive watch." She held it up for her to see.

"Oh, my Lord, where did you say you found the watch?" Nana asked, as if she had seen a ghost.

"I found it near the old cemetery." As soon as she saw Nana's face, Katie knew that Nana knew who the watch belonged to, and she knew there was a story behind it. "Whose watch is this, Nana?" she asked with some hesitation.

Nana's face flushed. She had to sit down.

"Nana, are you okay? Can I get you anything?" Katie asked

as she walked to the sink to get Nana a drink of water. After she handed her the glass, Nana drank all of it.

"Kat, I will tell you about the watch later this afternoon. Right now, you need to get to school."

Katie knew it was getting late, so she grabbed her backpack and headed out the door. She was a little reluctant to leave, but as she pulled out of the driveway, she looked back in her rearview mirror and saw Nana waving goodbye.

When she was in her second class that day, Katie was called to the principal's office. Nana had had another heart attack they said. Katie needed to get to the hospital.

Katie grabbed her stuff out of her locker and flew out the door to her car. She drove faster than she should have to the hospital and arrived in record time. She didn't even stop to think her driving could have put her in the hospital next to her grandmother. She arrived in time for nurses to tell her Nana was coming out of surgery and would be in recovery soon. She knew she wouldn't be able to see Nana for a few hours, so Katie headed to the chapel and knelt before God. She asked him to keep her nana safe and let her come out of this situation okay.

As she prayed, she thought about the watch. *Did I put too much stress on her? Is that why she ended up in the hospital? Who does this watch belong to?*

Katie sat there for what seemed like an hour, when she heard a voice behind her. "Katie!"

It was her best friend, Jamie. She had heard the news about Katie's nana and came to the hospital to be with her.

"Oh, Jamie, I'm so worried about Nana," she said. "They said she is in recovery. Remember what I told you earlier about

the watch I found and how Nana acted when I showed it to her?
I might have done this to my grandmother." She started crying.

"Katie, you didn't do this. You're talking crazy!" Jamie said,
trying to calm her down.

They had to find out if Nana was okay, so they went to the
nurses' station.

"Who are you looking for?" a nurse asked.

"Naomi O'Reilly," she said.

"I'm sorry, Miss. We do not have anyone here by that name."

"I know my grandmother was admitted. I was speaking to
someone earlier who told me she was in recovery!" she said, her
voice rising.

The head nurse came out to see what all the commotion was
and asked Katie again who she was looking for.

"Naomi O'Reilly!" Katie said with more conviction.

"I'm not sure who you spoke with earlier, young lady, but
we do not have anyone here by that name."

Maybe she was going crazy. Nothing was making much
sense to her these days.

"Okay, O'Reilly, give it up! You did this to try to get out of
the calculus test, didn't you?" Jamie said with a grin on her face.

"No! Jamie, you know I don't joke when it comes to my
nana's health," she said angrily. "Jamie, there's a real problem
here. I was called out of school today because of my grandmother. I'm not sure of anything now. I need to go home and
see my nana. I need to make sure she's okay. Would you go with
me?" she asked.

"Of course, I will go with you, Katie. Let me park my car in
the back lot," she said, walking out of the hospital. "I will meet
you out front."

Katie went to the emergency parking area to get her car. When she drove out front to get Jamie, she saw Jamie get into a car with her boyfriend, Lee. Katie was disappointed. She knew Lee had a hold on Jamie, but she hadn't thought Jamie would leave her when she was so upset. She sat in the parking lot with her head on the steering wheel and let out a good cry. Katie thought about everything that had just taken place, and she thought about the watch. She thought about the guy at the restaurant. Nothing seemed to make any sense to her any more.

When Katie looked up, she realized it had gotten dark. She wasn't sure how long she had been sitting there, but she needed to get home and get some answers. Katie started her car and drove off toward home. She was a bit hungry, so she thought she would stop to get a sub from the corner store.

Just as she pulled up to the store, it closed. "Ugh, why is everything going wrong today?" she said, hitting her hand on the steering wheel. Nana was probably wondering why she wasn't home for dinner. Knowing Nana, she'd assumed Katie was at the library, working on her term paper for graduation.

Katie pulled into the driveway and noticed all the lights were off. She was disappointed. "Not only have I had a day from hell, but I can't confront my grandmother about anything. Not the watch or the so-called heart attack," she said with frustration.

As Katie got out of the car, an SUV drove by the house with the man of her dreams in the front seat. Although she wanted to chase the car down, knowing her luck, she would have gotten a flat tire, or he would have just disappeared.

As Katie entered the front door, she heard Teddy, her German shepherd, barking. He was there to greet her. "Hi, boy!" she said with a smile. Teddy could always cheer her up. She went to the closet to get him a treat. He started growling. "What's wrong, boy?" she asked. He barked and growled at her again. This time, he jumped up onto her chest and knocked her to the ground. "Bad boy!" she yelled. *All I need tonight is crap from my dog!*

Katie went to the door and put Teddy out in the yard. He kept growling at her, as if he didn't know who she was. She headed for the kitchen, when she heard him growl again. She went to the door to see if there was anyone outside. She couldn't see anyone, but she noticed the light pole was still in the yard. It had been knocked over two days ago, and the electric company hadn't been out to fix it yet. She ignored everything and went to the kitchen to get something to eat. On the kitchen table, she found a note from Nana. "Dear Katie, I was invited to go to bingo with Joyce. I won't be home until late tonight. Hope to win big! Love, Nana." So Nana *was* okay, just not here. Katie couldn't believe her luck, or lack of it.

Katie tried calling Jamie, but she wasn't home. She remembered how hungry she was so she made herself a peanut butter and jelly sandwich and grabbed a big glass of milk. She sat down at the kitchen table to eat when Teddy started scratching at the door to come in. She got up and let him inside, with the understanding, of course, that he would behave himself. She no sooner sat back down to eat when the phone rang. The unfamiliar number on the display meant the caller couldn't be anyone but a telemarketer, so Katie let the answering machine pick it up. Suddenly, she heard Jamie's voice.

"Katie, where are you? I waited in the parking lot for over an hour for you."

Beep. Katie rushed to answer the phone, but by the time she got to it, Jamie was gone. "Now what am I supposed to do? Should I try calling her back?" she asked herself out loud.

Katie dialed Jamie. A recording came on immediately that said, "The number you are trying to reach has either been changed or disconnected. Ask your operator for assistance." She tried again, thinking she had dialed the wrong number. Again, the recording came on with the same message.

Now who's playing games? she thought. *I wonder if Jamie is behind all this crazy stuff I've been going through.* Katie thought she would pay Jamie a visit. She went to the closet to get her purse and coat, when Teddy started growling at her again. He really didn't want her to leave the house, and she *was* tired, so Katie resigned herself to a night at home. She knew she wasn't going to get any answers that night, so she thought she would sit and watch some TV. Before she knew what had happened, she fell asleep.

It was two o'clock in the morning when Katie woke up in the chair. She saw Teddy cuddled up at the front door, guarding it as if his life depended on it. At the top of the stairs, Katie heard Nana snoring softly from her room, so she knew she was home and safe. Katie continued to her own room, climbed into bed and fell into a deep sleep.

After what seemed to be a long restless night, she heard her name being called.

"Katie! Katie, please wake up! Honey, please wake up, and talk to me."

She tried opening her eyes. They felt as if there were two heavy books on them. She heard her name being called again.

"Katie, honey, please wake up!"

It sounded like Nana's voice. She tried again. This time, her eyes fluttered a bit, and she saw a bit of sunshine peeking into her room.

"Oh, Katie, thank God. You're going to be okay," said Nana with relief.

She started getting up slowly, but she felt as if all the energy had been drained from her body. "Nana, where am I?" She somehow knew she wasn't in her bedroom. Her lips were cracked, and she needed water. They were hard to separate, and she was having a tough time talking.

"Katie, you're at St. Joseph's Hospital. You've been here for the last month, sweetheart," Nana said with tears rolling down her face.

"What happened to me?" she asked, not knowing what to believe.

"Katie, you were in a car accident on March 5. It's now April 6. You were working that night. It was icy, and you were almost home, when you slid into the light pole outside the house. I was so afraid I had lost you. You've been in a coma for the last month. The doctors said if you were going to come out of it, it would probably be a couple weeks. I don't want to think of what would have happened if you hadn't come out of it. Jamie has been here every day to visit. They even let Teddy into your room until he started growling at the nurses when they changed your IVs. Oh, Katie, I'm so happy you woke up, sweetheart. You gave me a good scare!"

Katie suddenly looked down at her wrist. Papa's watch was on it, just as it had been the day, he'd given it to her before he passed away. It was her favorite piece of jewelry, and she never left home without it. She was happy to see it on her wrist and even happier that it hadn't gotten broken during the accident. "Nana, Papa was with me. His watch kept me alive," She said with tears streaming down her face.

Nana gave Katie a big smile and said, "I knew Papa was with you. I talk to him every night and I asked him to watch over you. Remember, he would always say, 'Use your time wisely because there is no guarantee of tomorrow.' Thank God, this time there is a tomorrow. Dr. Brannish says that once you're awake, there's no need to wait any longer. After they've checked you over, tomorrow you're going home!

Nana and Katie held on to each other for a long time before letting go.

Katie looked around the room. It smelled of Lysol liquid cleaner. As she sat there thinking, she knew she had to find out who had come into the restaurant the night of her accident. She couldn't get him off her mind. She wondered if he was the boy who had just moved into the house next to the Sampsons. The place had been vacant for years because the people in town knew of H.G. Sampson's reputation. He was one of the sharpest men in town, however, he was also one of the cruelest. Katie had heard from Jamie about the trouble at school with the Sampson boy. Jamie knew everything that went on at school and kept Katie informed.

Jamie had always been there for Katie. She had been there when her father had died of a heart attack and the day her mother had been admitted to the loony bin, as Katie referred to it. Nana didn't like it when Katie called the sanitarium a loony bin. Linda, Katie's mom, had gone to pieces after Katie's father passed away. She had been admitted the night Katie found her on the bathroom floor with her arms slashed. She had known her mother took pills and drank too much, but she never had thought she would do anything like that. Thank God the knife hadn't been sharp. It hadn't done too much damage—except it had helped to put her mother away. At least she could no longer hurt herself.

Katie had gone to visit her mother once, and Linda had kept asking where Katie's father was and when he was going to come see her. Katie had told her that he wasn't coming to see her and that he was dead. Her mother had screamed at the top of her lungs, and staff had come in with a tranquilizer to calm her down. Katie had decided she wasn't going to visit her mother again for a while.

Katie wanted out of the hospital. She knew she had a lot of work ahead of her if she intended to graduate in the spring. She desperately wanted to get back to a normal life. Then again, was anything in her life normal? After her mother had been committed, Katie had gone to live with her nana. She thought of her mother. What had gone so wrong? She was a beautiful woman with a gorgeous home, and the best part of her life was being a mom. At least that was what Katie had thought before she tried to commit suicide.

Katie loved living with her nana. Two years ago, after Papa passed, Nana had become depressed. Papa always had kept Nana busy with something or other. He had been a strong, intimidating man. He had been old school and thought that women belonged in the kitchen. Papa had had diabetes, and at first, he had taken care of himself. However, after a while, he had given up, gone back to drinking, and finally had to get his legs amputated after neuropathy set in. Papa had gone downhill ever since. He had given up on life. He always had said, "There is no use for a man to stick around if he can't take care of his family." He had felt he was half the man he used to be. He had kept a .38 Lady Colt next to his bed in case an intruder broke into the house. Unfortunately, Papa had used it on himself.

Some days, Katie had thought Nana might use it on him. He had been unbearable to live with after surgery. He constantly had barked orders at Nana and could be cruel sometimes. She wondered if Nana had ever really loved him or had just stayed married because of her religion. Katie remembered one thing her papa had told her: "Live fast, die young, and have a great-looking corpse." She never had liked that saying. Papa's fast living had put him in an early grave.

Katie sat at the end of the bed, waiting for Nana to arrive. She was so excited she could hardly control her emotions. Just then, the door flew open. It was the doctor. Katie looked disappointed.

"Hey, don't look so sad; they're right behind me," Dr. Brannish said.

Jamie came running around the doctor with Nana right behind her. She had a beautiful bouquet of flowers and balloons in her hand.

"C'mon, O'Reilly. Let's blow this popsicle stand," Jamie said, giggling.

Katie couldn't think of a better thing to say, so she got up and headed for the door.

"Hold on, Missy. You need to be wheeled out of here," said Dr. Brannish.

"Do I have to, Doc? I have been here long enough. Can't I just get up and go?" Katie begged.

"No, it's hospital policy. No patients leave this hospital walking. Everyone gets wheeled out. If you give me a minute, I will personally wheel you out myself," he said with a grin.

"How can I refuse that offer—my doctor giving me a ride out?" she said with a smile.

Jamie looked at Katie with her eyebrows raised. "C'mon, O'Reilly. You have got to be one of the happiest girls around. The cutest doctor in town is wheeling his patient out, and that patient just happens to be my best friend." She grinned.

"Don't be crazy, Jamie. That doctor could be my father!" Katie said, rolling her eyes at Jamie.

"Yes, Dummy, but he might have a son our age!" Jamie said, winking at her. Katie and Jamie sat there giggling. Just then, the doctor came into the room.

"What are you two giggling about?"

"Oh, nothing," they said in unison. Nana just looked at both girls and rolled her eyes.

"Is my patient ready to go?" Dr. Brannish asked.

"You have no idea how long I have been waiting to get out of here. I'm just glad I made it before graduation," Katie said, looking at Jamie.

"Thank you, Doctor, for taking such good care of my granddaughter," Nana said with teary eyes.

"If all my patients were as good as your granddaughter, I would be out of business. She was easy to care for, Naomi," Dr. Brannish said with a smile.

Is he flirting with my grandmother? Katie thought. *She is a beautiful woman.*

They all walked out together, with Dr. Brannish wheeling Katie through the doors. Dr. Brannish looked at Katie as they neared the door.

"Katie, remember to take it easy for the next couple days; you just got out of a coma. A little bump on your head could land you right back in here."

She nodded as they waved goodbye and went out the door.

CHAPTER 2

Hugh

H.G. Sampson was in his study, wondering when good ole Jack Knapp was going to show up. He hated every inch of Jack. If he had been honest with himself, he would have realized it was jealousy. Jack had it all. He had a beautiful wife, he was a good-looking guy, and he had a decent family—unlike H.G.'s little bastard son, who managed to get into trouble every time he turned around. Peter was always causing trouble. At least he had his other children. He knew Tony, Edith, and Tommy would go places. H.G. had warned Peter that if he didn't straighten up, he was going to send him to his uncle's house in California.

Kimberly, H.G.'s wife, came into the study with rage on her face. "I swear that kid has all your genes. He will never grow up to be anything because he will be just like you!" she said with spit coming out of her mouth. She was drunk. She started at nine o'clock in the morning, and by noon, she was plastered.

Kimberly was getting on H.G.'s last nerve. He thought about strangling her. He would have if he could have gotten away with it.

She screamed, "It's all your fault, you son of a bitch! Your kids hate you! You don't know how to be a father! You look out for you and only you! You're a selfish ingrate! A two-timing, lowlife—"

Smack. H.G. hit Kimberly so hard she fell to the floor. "I'm done with you; you're a stupid bitch. You don't care about your children or the way you look or smell. Now get your ass off my floor and out of my study! If you ever come barging in on me again, I'll—"

"You'll what? Kill me like you did your father?" Kimberly said with as much force as she dared. She knew that would strike a nerve, and she held her head down, waiting for the next hit.

"Get out of here, woman! You're going to regret what you just said."

Kimberly backed out of the room as fast as she could, looked back, and yelled, "Burn in hell, you dirty bastard!"

She ran down the hallway, stopping to make sure H.G. didn't follow her. She leaned up against the wall when she knew the coast was clear and slid down it. She thought of ways to kill herself. She didn't want to be with H.G. anymore. Or, she thought, she could kill him and get away with it.

Kimberly got up and ran to the bathroom. Leaning over the toilet, she vomited furiously. She couldn't believe she was even thinking that way. She wasn't a criminal, and just thinking about murder made her vomit some more. What would her dear ole mother have thought of her now? She had put H.G. on a pedestal, although she didn't think too much of her mother. Her mother hadn't gotten rid of that son-of-a-bitch boyfriend who had molested Kimberly when she was a child.

Kimberly didn't know what she was going to do. All she knew was that she needed to get away from H.G. before he killed her.

H.G. was furious. He had to get rid of her. The drunker she got, the mouthier she became. She was more trouble than she was worth. He had kept her around all these years because of the kids. Now that the kids were old enough to take care of themselves, he thought it might be time to replace her. But it wasn't going to be easy. With Peter in trouble because of Jack Knapp's kid and with H.G.'s own past, the police would be watching him closer than ever.

He thought about Peter and how much he reminded H.G. of himself. *Damn kid's a troublemaker.* How was he going to get his kid off from an assault charge, when the one he had assaulted was a town cop's kid?

H.G. Sampson had been born Hugh Gregory Sampson on December 12, 1958, to Peter and Wilma Sampson. H.G. had lived in fear most of his life. He was a scared boy underneath the powerful aura he promoted on the outside.

His father was a dairy farmer who lived by specific rules: the power of hands and a good whip. He beat his children like he beat his animals. According to one story, one day Peter Sampson got so angry with one of his cows that he punched it right between the eyes and killed it. They said he was so strong he could pick up a two-hundred-pound cow and toss it around as if it were a kitten. When he was mad, Peter Sampson was a man you didn't want to be around.

Peter worked hard all his life, and he expected the same of his children. He and Wilma had three boys: Peter Jr., Denny, and Hugh. Peter Jr. was a disappointment. He got a girl pregnant at seventeen, so Peter Sr. sent him and his new bride-to-be to California to live with an uncle. Peter Sr. had high hopes for Denny, but those hopes were short-lived. Denny was a big partier. He was out one night, drinking and driving, and hit a dump truck head-on while drag racing. He was killed instantly. Hugh was the only son left at home. Hugh was a scrawny little guy with acne scars. Peter didn't have much hope for him.

Peter started working Hugh to death. By the time he was sent off to college, Hugh was fitter than any kid around. He was the quarterback of his high school football team and ranked first in nationals in wrestling. Not that he needed it, but he received a full scholarship to Penn State.

Hugh didn't want to go back to farming after graduating college, but when his father got sick, he was forced to take over his business. His father mysteriously died in his sleep one night, and the local rumor was that Hugh had finally killed his father. Wilma was so heartbroken that she passed on not long after Peter. Thus, Hugh was left to run the family farm. He hired a lot of hands to do the dirty work while he studied law and real estate. By the time Hugh was thirty, he owned half the town, purchasing everything that came up for sale. Some even said he owned the police department.

Hugh was a decent man back then. He was engaged to be married to his high school sweetheart, Melinda Moyer. However, the night before the wedding, Hugh got drunk, and Melinda found him the next morning with his best man's girlfriend, Kimberly. Hugh tried to tell Melinda that Kimberly didn't mean anything to him. He hadn't known what he was doing. However, when it turned out Kimberly was pregnant, Melinda moved to Chicago to be with her grandparents. Hugh was forced to marry Kimberly to save face.

Hugh became bitter. Peter was born, and Kimberly thought Hugh would be a nicer man, but Peter was a constant reminder of the love of his life who'd gotten away. As a result, he wasn't nice to Peter. Kimberly got pregnant again with another son. Tony was the apple of Hugh's eye. He wasn't a reminder of sorrow, as Peter was. Then Edith, his baby girl, was born, and finally, by accident, Tommy was born. They all grew up spoiled, or so people thought. Hugh was hardest on Peter, though. Peter was in constant trouble. The fight with the Knapp kid was the last straw. After everything settled down, he would send Peter to live with his aunt and uncle in California. They had been asking for the kids to come stay with them. Now they could have their wish. At least one of his kids.

Edith called her aunt and uncle almost every night, crying. Her parents argued so much that she wanted to go live with her aunt and uncle. Her mother drank too much, and she didn't think her father really loved her mother. The things he said to her were horrible.

In the beginning, Kimberly asked H.G. to get help with his drinking, but after years of putting up with his drinking, she thought, *if you can't beat them, you might as well join them.* She became an ugly drunk. One-night Kimberly was so drunk she passed out on the floor. They thought she was dead. She went to the hospital only to find out she had pancreatitis. She thought this was going to be her escape. She would die if she didn't quit drinking. The only thing that saved her was her children.

However, she didn't stop completely. After she found out Peter hurt the Knapp kid, she started drinking again. She knew he was going to end up just like his father. He thought he could do anything to anyone and get away with it. What was she going to do?

CHAPTER 3

Jack

Tina sat by the bay window, looking out at the trees. Spring was in the air. She always liked that time of year. Everything was waking up from the cold winter. Flowers were blooming, trees were budding, and the birds were starting to come back.

Tina and Jack had been married for eighteen years. They had two sons: J.T. and Tobin. J.T. was tall for his age and handsome. Tobin was skinny and small for his age. Tobin had been sick most of his life. He was allergic to everything it seemed. He was constantly in and out of hospitals. That was why Tina had had to go back to work in retail. Jack's working at the police station didn't bring in enough money to pay all the hospital bills.

J.T. was athletic and played sports in school. Tobin liked to sit around and read or play video games. J.T. had high aspirations. He wanted to go off to college after high school to play football. Tobin wasn't sure what he wanted to be when he grew up. He was in the tenth grade, and his brother was a senior that year. Tobin would sit around for hours, asking his mother what he should do when he finished school. Tina kept telling Tobin he could do anything he put his mind to. She always felt guilty when talking to Tobin. She felt she hadn't paid much attention to her son, and now look where he was going. She wasn't sure. When J.T. was little, Tina didn't have to work. Unfortunately, with all the medical bills from Tobin's illnesses, she had to work to help keep their house.

Tina's days were filled with stocking shelves, and arranging new merchandise for displays. She was one of the department managers at the local retail store. She hoped for an assistant manager's position before too long. Rumor had it that the current assistant manager was going to get her own store, and Tina was next in line for the assistant managers position there. She hated working holidays, and weekends were tough sometimes too. However, Mr. Sampson was a stickler for anyone working for him. If a person was in management, that person had better make sure he or she didn't have too much of a personal life. She knew that H.G. Sampson was tougher on his management staff. She would soon find out how tough. As a department manager, she didn't have too much contact with him, but as assistant manager, she would find out she needed to work longer hours and harder hours than she was already. She knew a little about H.G., especially some of the rumors. Apparently, a few years ago, H.G. had run over a young girl while out drinking one night and killed her. When the time for his trial had come and he'd faced going to jail, his blood alcohol report had gone missing. The entire town had been in an uproar. This was proof that money could, indeed, buy everything.

Tina came from a small family. It was just her, her mother, and her sister. She wasn't used to being around all males before she and Jack were married. She had called her mother every other day when J.T. was little. She had wanted to know how to stop the baby from constantly peeing on her. Her mother had laughed and told her she needed to be quicker at changing his diapers. By the time Tobin had been born, she had become a pro.

Jack had been with the police department ever since he'd graduated from the police academy. He'd had high hopes in following his high school football career. However, after graduation, Jack's dream was crushed when he went camping with a few buddies one weekend. They had gone rappelling, the snap had broken, and Jack had fallen ninety feet to the ground and broken several bones in his body. His football career was over. He was lucky to be alive. Jack had had to go through physical therapy to learn how to walk again. That was where he'd met Tina, who'd been working as a nurse's aide at the hospital. Two months into his therapy, Jack and Tina were engaged to be married. A year later, J.T. was born. Jack's parents didn't like the fact that Tina was Catholic. Only after J.T. was born had they had anything to do with the couple. Marion Knapp wanted to be in her grandson's life. However, Jack still held a grudge over the fact his parents hadn't attended their wedding, so Tina had to sneak visits with Marion.

Tina sat watching *The Morning Show* on TV, when the phone rang. She immediately thought it was the school calling about Tobin. However, this time, it was about J.T. He had gotten into a fight with the Sampson kid. The secretary was calling to let her know they were taking J.T. to the hospital. Tina went into a panic attack. She picked up the phone and dialed the police station. Sherry, the receptionist, answered the phone.

"Hey, Sherry, it's Tina. Is Jack around?" she asked, barely controlling her emotions.

"Tina, the school called Jack to let him know about J.T. You can probably catch him at the hospital," Sherry said.

"Thanks. I will."

"Do you want me to get ahold of him for you, Tina?" Sherry asked, concerned about the way Tina was acting.

"No, I will meet him at the hospital. Thanks again, Sherry."

Tina grabbed her jacket and her cell phone to call her mother. She thought about calling Marion but didn't want to upset Jack.

When Tina arrived at the hospital, Jack and his partner, Johnny, were there. She ran into Jack's arms and nearly fainted.

"Have you eaten yet today, Tina?" Jack knew the answer but asked anyway.

"No, I had a cup of coffee. That's not important. How's J.T.?" she asked, a little winded.

"The doctor said he will be fine. He had to get stitches. We can see him after they finish stitching him up," Jack said, annoyed with Tina. Jack knew his wife was bulimic. Trying to get her to eat and keep it in her stomach was another thing.

"Oh, thank God!" Tina said with tears rolling down her cheeks.

"Johnny, can you get me a cup of coffee? I need to talk to Tina for a minute."

Johnny walked away, and Jack looked right at Tina. "You know, you're going to end up in the hospital right next to your son, or even worse," Jack said, knowing her obsession with her weight was a big problem. If she didn't gain weight, she would end up in the hospital or die.

"Can we discuss this later? I don't need this bullshit right now, Jack," Tina said without looking at him. She walked over to the sofa and sat down. *Why would J.T. get into a fight with Peter Sampson? Especially when J.T. and Tony are friends? I wonder if it has anything to do with that girl.* Tina felt as if she was going to faint and knew she wouldn't get any sympathy from Jack. Jack had been on her a lot lately about getting help. She had plugged up all the toilets in their house more times than she cared to admit.

Just then, a nurse came out to tell Tina and Jack they could go in to see J.T. Tina got up from the couch and fell to the floor.

Jack came running over to his wife. "Tina, get up, honey!"

The nurse came over to see what was happening. Jack told the nurse that Tina was a sick woman and probably just needed to get something to eat. The nurse had smelling salts in her scrubs, and she put some under Tina's nose. She started waking up. Tina looked around and apologized. She looked at Jack for some sympathy, but he wasn't about to give her any.

Tina had quit purging when she was carrying the boys, but as soon as she delivered them, she went right back to it. She had always been an active person. She was five foot nine and weighed a hundred pounds. She was always complaining about her weight.

Tina looked away in shame when she saw Jack glaring at her. "Let's go see J.T. I will be all right," she said, reassuring the nurse.

They opened the door to the recovery room. J.T. was sitting

on the bed with his head bandaged as if he were a wounded soldier. Jack was the first to speak.

"What happened, Son?" he asked with authority.

J.T. knew he was in big trouble when his dad talked in that tone of voice. "Peter Sampson came after me in the parking lot because I was picking on him about his choice of friends. Everyone thinks he's using this one girl for sex. So, I called him on it. He got mad at me and came after me like a madman. So, I said something to him," J.T. said, looking down at the floor. J.T. knew he was in the wrong but thought everyone at school was laughing at his ignorance. "Peter didn't like what I said, came after me, and smashed my head on the parking lot. Now I'm here." He looked at his mother for help.

Tina was empathetic but wasn't happy with J.T. Jack looked at J.T. and said he would have to find out what Peter Sampson had to say. Just then, the doctor came into the room.

"We are going to keep J.T. overnight for observation. He has a concussion and needs to be watched a little more carefully tonight," the doctor said.

"Okay, Doctor," they said together.

Jack left the room to find Johnny. He was going to have a talk with Peter Sampson. He wanted to get his side of the story. Johnny was sitting in the waiting room.

"C'mon, Johnny. We are going to talk with the Sampson boy."

Tina told J.T. everything would be okay. She told him she loved him and would be back to see him later. Tina walked out of the hospital and got into her car. She wasn't feeling well and knew she probably should wait to drive. She didn't see the truck coming straight at her. By the time the ambulance got to her, she was dead.

H.G. saw the patrol car pulling into the driveway. Johnny Matters was driving, and Jack Knapp was in the passenger seat. He knew Jack was going to be hard on his boy, and at that point, he didn't care. He was going to send Peter to his uncle's house as soon as the dust cleared. The doorbell rang, and Cindy, the maid, answered it.

"Is H.G. here, Cindy?" Jack asked, knowing his vehicle was in the driveway.

"Yes, sir, he is in his study. I will let him know you're here," Cindy said as she turned to get H.G.

Cindy had been with the Sampsons for years. She had seen and heard a lot of stuff that went on. She even thought she would write a book about the Sampsons one day. Well, it was her leverage if she ever came into trouble and needed money.

Cindy walked off to the kitchen, but before she did, she offered the men a drink. They both declined because they were on duty. H.G. stepped into the foyer and asked what they were doing there. Jack opened his mouth, but Johnny stepped in front of him.

"H.G., I'm sure you've heard what went on at school today. We are here to talk to Peter and find out what he has to say," Johnny said, glaring at Jack to keep his mouth shut. By rights, Jack shouldn't have come with him.

"I don't even know where that boy of mine is, so you might as well leave," H.G. said gruffly.

"He will have to show up sooner or later, and when he does, you will let him know we need to talk with him, right, H.G.?" Jack said with an angry look.

H.G. was pissed. Why would he have hidden that little son of a bitch? He was nothing but trouble. H.G. led them to the door. "Good day, gentlemen," he said.

"You will let us know when you see him, H.G.?" Johnny said with authority.

"Yeah, I will tell him. I don't care what you do to that kid. He's had it coming for a while." He shut the door behind them.

As Johnny and Jack left the driveway, they received the call about Tina. Johnny threw the patrol lights on and headed back to the hospital. By the time they got there, Tina had been pronounced dead. Jack fell to the floor and started crying. He felt terrible about the way he had treated Tina earlier. What was he going to do now? How was he going to take care of the boys? He had to go get Tobin from school. He asked Johnny if he could go pick up Tobin at school and bring him back to the hospital. That way, he could tell both boys at the same time. Johnny said he would get Tobin and asked Jack if he needed anything else. He felt bad for him.

"No, thanks, Johnny. This is going to be hard enough," he said, wiping tears from his face.

He went to talk to the EMT who had brought Tina into the hospital. George was the emergency management technician who had picked up Tina.

"Hey, George, can you tell me anything about the accident?" Jack asked.

"Not really, Jack. I won't know anything until the autopsy is done. All I can tell you is that she must have passed out or fallen asleep. Her car hit the semitruck head-on. The truck was going westbound, the opposite direction of the way she was going," George said sympathetically.

Jack knew by George's statement that Tina's bulimia finally had gotten the best of her. He needed to find the medical examiner to let him know what he knew. Just then, he saw the patrol car pull up into the emergency entrance. Tobin ran into the hospital. Jack grabbed him and hugged his son.

"Daddy, what's going on with J.T.? I heard some kids talk about him at school," Tobin said, wide-eyed.

"Tobin, let's go see your brother," Jack said, taking Tobin's hand.

They walked to his room, where J.T. was sitting in his bed, eating his lunch.

"J.T., Tobin, I have some bad news," Jack said, starting to get teary-eyed. "Your mother was in an accident. She's no longer with us, guys." His voice was barely audible.

"What are you trying to say, Dad?" J.T. asked, not believing what he was hearing. Tobin just stood there staring into space.

"Mom's dead, J.T.," his father said with tears running down his face.

Tobin started screaming. "No, not my mommy!" He screamed so loudly that nurses and doctors ran into the room.

"Oh, Jack, we didn't know who was in here. Sorry to hear, Jack. If you want, I can give something to your son to calm him down," Dr. Brannish said.

"Thanks, Doctor. I think that's a good idea."

Tobin kept screaming and yelling. The doctor came in with a tranquilizer. He gave a shot to Tobin. J.T. was just staring at the wall at that point, not wanting to believe his father. His head started pounding. He let the doctor know, and the doctor gave the nurse orders to get him some medicine. It didn't take long to take effect, and soon J.T. was sleeping.

Jack had a lot of work ahead of him. He thanked the doctor, called his mother, and took Tobin home.

CHAPTER 4

Edith

Graduation was coming closer, and Katie started her internship with the Victims' Advocacy Center. She would be working at the hospital, counseling kids at the Behavioral Science Unit.

She knew all about the watch. She knew she could help some people, and others she couldn't, because evil was real, and the watch only worked on certain people.

What if you found out that a choice you made would change your destiny? Would you take it, or would you walk away?

The first encounter she had with the watch was with a girl named Edith. She was a little redhead with the biggest green eyes Katie had ever seen. Katie had just started interning at the Behavioral Science Unit the day she spoke with Edith. Edith Sampson was from a disturbed family. Katie had heard rumors about Edith's father, but she knew nothing about her mother. Edith found herself in the BSU due to her drinking a whole bottle of vodka to try to ease the pain of her parents arguing. She didn't realize she could have killed herself from alcohol poisoning. Or maybe she did realize it and wanted to leave the environment she was in. When Katie sat down to talk with Edith, Edith was a little hesitant to open up to Katie, but eventually she started talking. Soon they were chatting as if they were old girlfriends.

"Katie, I don't want to be an alcoholic like my mother. I'm just so tired of my parents constantly battling each other for no reason," Edith said with tears rolling down her face.

"Have you tried talking to them"? Katie asked.

"More times than I care to admit. My mother blames my father for everything me and my brothers do, especially when we get into trouble. My father is always telling my mother she's a no-good drunk. He is relentless! I don't know how she puts up with his vulgarity. He's not helping my mother. I think that's why she drinks so much. She's afraid of him most of the time, until she starts drinking. After she's completely inebriated, that's when she mouths off, and they begin to argue like crazy. It's every day. How am I supposed to live with them? I started drinking a few weeks ago at a party. At first, I was afraid I was going to get into trouble. But after a while, my mother told me how I could sneak vodka in my water bottles that I take to school. She told me, 'If you can't beat them, you might as well join them,'" she told Katie, crying harder.

"Why haven't you spoken to any of your friends about this problem you're having, Edith"? Katie asked.

"I don't have any close friends. They're all afraid of my parents. One day in the eighth grade, I brought my friend Georgia home to meet my mom. Mom did nothing but tell her that her parents were no-good white trash. So, my friends don't visit me anymore." She put her head down in embarrassment.

"How are you doing in school, Edith?" Katie asked.

"I can barely make it through the day without taking a drink. Katie, I'm afraid. I don't want to be a drunk. I don't want to end up like my mother. She's miserable, and she doesn't like her life. I wish I never took a drink that night. I wish I had a redo."

Suddenly, Papa's watch started spinning counterclockwise, and the hourglass on the watch's face, turned upside down. Katie was no longer at the BSU. She was looking through a window at Edith being yelled at by her teacher for not getting her homework done. Edith just stared at the blackboard. The bell rang, and she went to collect her books and her backpack. She had a big smile on her face. That night was the night of the party, the one where she had taken her first drink. She had gotten a do-over! She was walking to her car, and she saw Katie in the parking lot. She smiled at her. Katie walked up to Edith to let her know that while she remembered right now, she would not remember later that any of this had happened. She was going to have to make a choice again if she wanted to stay away from alcohol.

"I'm going to do the right thing, Katie. I know I will," Edith said.

"Just remember, you make the decision to drink; no one else does that for you. You will know there is something different about your choice, but you won't remember us. Try to make the right choice this time, Sweetie."

Katie walked away. Edith was happy. She jumped into her

car and decided she wasn't going to go to the party that night. She had a new outlook on life. She wasn't going to let her parents' arguing get to her. She would ask her dad if she could go live with her aunt and uncle in California.

CHAPTER 5

Georgia

Katie found herself back at the BSU. Although Edith wouldn't remember what had taken place after tomorrow, Katie would. In the children's ward she was introduced to Georgia. Georgia was a tall girl with curly blonde hair and a look of sadness that was hard to hide. Georgia was at the BSU because her grandmother had walked into the bathroom to find Georgia cutting herself. Her boyfriend, Jeremy, had just passed away. In her brokenness, Georgia felt that the physical pain could possibly take away the crushing emotional pain she felt. She knew nothing else to help her deal with the pain other than to cut herself.

Georgia looked up at Katie and asked who she was.

"I'm Katie O'Reilly. I'm here helping the staff out," she told Georgia. "What brings you in here?"

"My grandmother ratted me out. I just lost my boyfriend, Jeremy, last month in a car wreck. My grandmother found out

I was cutting and told my parents. Now I'm stuck in here for who knows how long," she told Katie with anger in her eyes.

"Do you want to tell me about Jeremy?" Katie asked.

"Where should I start? He's gone now. I don't know how I'm going to live without him," Georgia said with tears in her eyes.

"Why don't you tell me about how you met Jeremy?" Katie said cautiously, and Georgia agreed.

"Well, we were both in the seventh grade when Jeremy and his mom moved here. We got put together for a project in art class. From then on, we started talking to each other and spending all our time together. We were going to get married after graduation. Jeremy wanted to go into the military. I was going to be his wife. Now I'm not sure what I'm going to do. I'm scared, and I feel so lost, Katie," she said, crying. "I should have gone to that party with Jeremy. The night he died he got into a fight with his mom. She didn't want Jeremy to go into the military. She wanted him to go to college. So, he was upset anyway. I didn't feel like going to a party that was going to have people there I didn't get along with, so I told him I had homework to do. He got drunk and drove home. Unfortunately, he never made it home. He lost control of his car on a curve and hit a tree head-on. Now he's gone, and I don't want to go on without him. I should have gone to the party with him. I should have never let him go." She started crying harder.

Katie was sort of expecting her papa's watch to move, but she knew that once someone died, he or she was gone forever.

"I'm so sorry, Georgia. I know that sorry won't bring Jeremy back, but I believe you didn't go with him because you still have a journey called life that you've got to live. You're here for some reason. Jeremy wouldn't want to see you hurting yourself, would he?" Katie said.

"No, he would be angry with me if he knew what I was doing," Georgia said with a deeper sadness.

"I know one way to help you, Georgia. Wear a rubber band around your wrist, and every time you feel the need to cut yourself, snap it hard. That will remind you that Jeremy wouldn't want to see you hurting yourself in the way you're doing right now. Or you could always take a red pen and write on your leg with it. Make scratch marks on your thighs. Sometimes that also reminds us of what we are doing." Katie had learned those techniques during training.

"Thank you for listening to me, Katie. I appreciate it," Georgia said with a little smile on her face.

"Well, you're meeting with Dr. Faulk this evening, right?" Katie asked, and Georgia said yes. "He's really nice and a very good doctor. He will find a way to help you. I'm sure of that." She smiled at Georgia. "My shift is ending today, but I will be back tomorrow. If you'd like, we can talk some more," Katie told her as she grabbed her briefcase.

"Okay, I will see you tomorrow," Georgia said with a bigger smile.

"Yes, you will, and have a good night, Georgia."

"Thanks, Katie!"

Katie walked out of the room and swiped her badge to get into the breakroom. Her coat was in her locker. She grabbed the coat and started heading for the elevator. Just then, Papa's watch started burning her arm—not like a fire burn, just a warm burning like the sun through an afternoon window. She wasn't sure why she was getting the feeling, but she hurried down the elevator and out to her car. The air was fresh, and the sun beamed down onto her face. She wondered how Edith was making out with her parents. She also felt guilty about not being able to help Georgia. *How many other kids am I going to encounter that I won't be able to help?* She got into her little yellow Cobalt, the car her friends had dubbed Bumblebee. Even with 125,000 miles on it, it ran like a kitten. She couldn't do anything else that night, so she drove home. The drive wasn't long, but she was tired.

CHAPTER 6

The Hospital

The following day at the BSU, Katie was shown to a girl named Paula. Paula was rocking back and forth in a chair in the corner. Katie went to talk to Paula and immediately felt Papa's watch burn her arm. She knew that wasn't a good sign but thought she would try to understand why.

"Hi, Paula. I'm Katie. It seems there is something wrong, and I'd like to try to help you. Can we talk?" Katie asked.

Paula shrugged.

Katie wanted to run. Papa's watch was getting hotter. Katie looked into Paula's eyes, and she swore she saw black coal.

"What brings you here?" Paula asked Katie.

"I'm with the Victims' Advocacy Center. I'm what they call a medical advocate." Katie wasn't sure why, but she felt something was off about Paula. "So, do you want to talk? Or do you want me to sit here with you?"

"I want you to listen, but if you're here to preach to me, I want you to go."

Just then, the lunch bell rang. Paula got up off her seat, looked back at Katie, and said, "Next time, bitch, you might want to try to save someone else. Too late for me."

Katie got up and walked to the bathroom. She ran water in the sink and threw some onto her face. *Papa, what am I doing? I'm not strong enough for this job.* Looking into the mirror, she noticed her eyes were bloodshot.

Suddenly, the door to the bathroom flew open and hit the back of the wall. Paula was standing in the doorway. "Shame your eyes have gotten so bloodshot. If you know what's good for you, you will mind your own business and leave us alone!"

Katie walked past Paula and again felt the watch burn her arm. During lunch, she tried calling her nana. She needed to get some answers. Unfortunately, it was Thursday, and Nana was at bingo. Katie talked to her supervisor, told her she wasn't feeling well, and said she would be back in the morning. Usually, she stayed an hour after lunch, but Paula's attitude made her feel sick to her stomach, and she needed to speak with her grandmother about the burning sensation in her arm.

Katie went to the breakroom to retrieve her jacket from her locker. As she looked down the hall, she saw Paula waving goodbye to her. She swiped her badge to the breakroom and grabbed her coat. All she could think about was getting away from there. Then she walked to the elevator and swiped her badge again to go downstairs to freedom.

The air was cool for that time of the year. The Northeast was usually warmer at the end of April. When she was younger, by the time May came around, she was wearing shorts to school. Not that year.

She walked to her car. She couldn't get there fast enough. She opened the door and put her briefcase and purse in the front seat. She looked up for some reason and spotted Paula looking out the window, smiling at her. Katie felt the warm feeling of the watch again. She got into her car and put her head down on the steering wheel. *What am I doing? This one seems to be evil. Something's off about this girl*, she thought. She turned the key to her car and drove home. Her body was shaking uncontrollably. She didn't understand any of it. When she finally pulled into the driveway, she didn't spot Nana's car. She walked into the house and yelled out for Nana out of habit. She knew she wouldn't get an answer. She climbed the stairs to her bedroom. Katie threw her stuff onto her bed and started crying. *Papa, why have you given me this responsibility? I can't do this.* She fell asleep, crying.

Katie wasn't sure how much time had passed when she heard Nana come back into the house.

"Nana, can we talk? Something strange happened at the BSU today, and I really need to talk to you about it."

"Katie, before you go any further, I have to tell you something. I know you think you can't handle the responsibilities the watch brings, but if Papa chose you, you were the right one for the job. He mentioned it when you turned four. Do you remember the day we were out walking near the park, and you fell off the street curb and almost got hit by a car? He knew as soon as you told him that you weren't going to die, as you had too much to live for. He knew your spirit and the size of your heart. He was sure you were destined to wear the watch. However, if you're looking for answers, there are some notebooks your grandfather left in the basement. You should take the time to read them. I'm not the person you need to ask for those answers. I wasn't involved with too much of your grandfather's helping other people. He kept most of that to himself. It helped me cope with the whole thing."

Katie suddenly heard her nana yelling for her to come down for supper. She knew she had been dreaming again. Nana was in the kitchen starting dinner when Katie walked in. There were many questions she wanted to ask, but she felt she would be putting too much stress on her grandma, so she decided she would wait.

"Nana, can I help you with anything?"

Nana was making lasagna and asked Katie to get the garlic out of the refrigerator. Katie knew that Nana always made garlic bread when she made any Italian dishes. She knew exactly how her nana liked the garlic cut: almost minced. She grabbed a clove out of the fridge and started cutting it. She looked up at her grandmother for just a second and the knife slipped. Katie cut the top of her finger off, along with the tip of her fingernail. The cut was bleeding badly, so she ran it under water in the sink. Nana grabbed the paper towels and wrapped it up.

"Let's get you to the emergency room, Katie. You did a number on that finger." She grabbed more paper towels, but the cut bled through the towels.

They got into the car and drove to the ER. The nurse at registration looked at Katie's finger and checked her right in. She wanted to know how the cut had happened and asked when Katie had gotten a tetanus shot. She brought a cup full of coppery liquid over to the table. She told Katie it was iodine and said to soak her finger in it. Katie told her she just had gotten a tetanus shot before she started working at the hospital and told her how she had hurt herself. She looked at Katie a little funny, as if she knew her.

"You're the new girl working upstairs, right?"

She knew Katie worked there but wanted to hear it from her. Katie told her she was and that she would need to get ahold of somebody to let them know about what had happened that night. She was due back in the morning. The nurse said she would get the doctor and then let her know if she could work in the morning.

The doctor came in and asked what had happened, and Katie let him know. "Well, Katie, you sure did a number on your finger. You'll need to take some antibiotics and pain medication for a few days. You're also going to have to soak your finger in iodine for the next week at least twice a day. Keep the finger bandaged until you start to see a scab. The nurse tells me you work upstairs. You're going to have to take tomorrow off."

She looked at him with disappointment.

"It's only one day, Katie. You don't work weekends, do you?"

"No, I only work week days."

"I will ask the nurse to let them know upstairs that you will be out until Monday. Remember to soak that finger, and take your medicine. You should heal up nicely. You will notice a numbness at the tip of your finger, but that is to be expected."

"Thank you, Doctor."

She jumped off the bed and went looking for Nana. She was ready to go home. An ambulance pulled up out front of the ER on her way out. Just then, Papa's watch started burning her arm. She knew George, the EMT on duty, and asked him if he could tell her who was in the ambulance.

"All I can tell you is it's a young boy. Approximately fifteen years old. His mother is a drunk and apparently threw a pot of hot water on him. We have the police coming into the ER so they can investigate. The kid was lucky a burn van was just down the street from where he lives, and they carry the new burn pads in their vehicle. The kid would look and feel worse than he already does had they not been there to put pads on him right away."

"Oh my God! What kind of mother would do such a thing?"

"A drunk, Katie."

As the stretcher was being wheeled into the emergency room, Katie noticed it was Tommy Sampson. Edith was right behind him. Katie froze. She couldn't move or say anything to anyone. Nana came walking out of the bathroom and noticed she was staring into space.

"Katie, are you, all right?"

Katie didn't answer right away.

"Kate, are you okay, sweetheart?"

This time, she used a little more volume to her voice. Its startled Katie. She turned around and told Nana she was fine. She then turned to George and asked if she could talk with Tommy.

"Not tonight, Katie. The boy is in a lot of pain. Children and Youth Services is coming in to speak with the family. I guess his father was out of the house at the time; he's been notified and is on his way. If you know anything about H.G. Sampson, you're better off if you're not around when he gets here."

Before Katie could say anything, Nana was behind her. "Katlyn Rae! You need to get home and take care of that finger, or you won't be good for anyone!"

Katie looked at George and rolled her eyes. "Okay, Nana, let's go."

They walked quietly to her car. As soon as they got into the vehicle, Katie turned to Nana to let her know about Edith.

"I just don't understand how I could have helped his sister, and now he's in trouble, and Papa's watch started burning my arm. It's almost like a warning. Every time I think of helping certain people, Papa's watch lets me know I can't or shouldn't."

"Yes, you are going to have times like that, Katie. Your papa let me know about some situations he was in when he couldn't help. He would get so angry. But in the end, the situations in which he couldn't help worked out better than if he had gotten involved. Just remember that, sweetie."

Katie resigned herself to the fact that maybe it was a situation she had little or no control over. She leaned against the window and sighed.

"I guess the lasagna will have to wait until tomorrow. Do you want to grab a pizza? I called ahead, knowing you'd never turn a pizza down."

"Thanks, Nana. Just what the doctor ordered." Katie giggled.

Nana parked in front of Papa C's; the restaurant Katie had worked at before her accident. Katie looked around, thinking maybe she could see the mysterious man she'd run into that night, but there was no sign of him anywhere. Then she thought about Edith. *How was it that I was able to help her, but I'm not going to be able to help her younger brother? I guess what Nana was saying makes sense.* Edith wanted some help for her mother. Now she was going to be forced to go into rehab. *It's just a shame that one person must suffer because of someone's evilness.* Tommy wouldn't forget the incident for the rest of his life. *I'd love to be a fly on the wall when H.G. gets to the hospital.*

Nana opened the back door and set the pizza down on the backseat. "Are you okay, Katie? Looks like I startled you. You must have been thinking about something deep."

"I was just wondering how people work, Nana."

"If you figure that out, you let me know. I have been asking the same question my whole life."

They sat silently the rest of the way home. Before long, Nana pulled into the driveway and parked the car in the garage. Katie could hear Teddy barking inside. Nana grabbed the pizza from the backseat and walked inside. Katie leaned her head on the dash. She wasn't ready to accept the fact that she couldn't help Tommy. She just couldn't wrap her head around the fact that his mother would do such a thing. *Will anything I do make a difference?*

CHAPTER 7

Best Friend

Katie woke up Monday morning refreshed and ready to take on the day. She couldn't remember her dream. If she'd had a nightmare, she was glad she didn't remember it. Unfortunately, Nana had left to volunteer for the local thrift shop down the street. Papa had left her in a good position when he passed, so she didn't have to go out and find a job, but Nana loved volunteering and helping others. Nana was a beautiful soul. Anyone who knew Katie's grandmother loved her. She had a smile that lit up the entire room when she walked into it.

The answering machine caught Katie's eye. It was blinking. *Someone must have called when I was in the shower.* It was her boss. She said the BSU had had something happen last night, and they were on complete lockdown that morning. Katie was just as happy. She needed to go to school and work on her term paper, which was due next week for her to graduate. *Plus, I haven't seen Jamie lately. I could catch up with her.* She decided she would go to the library.

Katie pulled into the school parking lot and shut off her car. Jamie was there when she got out.

"Katie, did you hear about the Sampson kid? His mother tried burning him alive! I guess they've locked her up in a sanitarium."

"Yeah, and she will become best friends with my mother!" They giggled together.

"What brings you here so early?" Jamie asked.

"Apparently, something happened at the BSU last night, and they're on lockdown."

"Probably that creepy girl you were talking about the other day did something. What's her name?"

"Jamie, you know I can't tell you that, and I'm not sure what her story is all about yet, so how about you give her a break?" She rolled her eyes at Jamie.

"A little touchy this morning, O'Reilly?"

"No. I just get worried about not being able to help people like I want to or like I'm put here to do."

They walked to the library together, not saying much more.

Though Jamie had been Katie's friend since the first grade, and they did everything together, you couldn't find two more different characters. Jamie was a small-minded person who often saw the dark side of people. She herself had grown up in a disturbed family, and most of her thinking was warranted. Her uncle had been put in jail after four drinking-while-driving incidents. Her grandfather had been placed in prison shortly after she was born because of extortion. Her brother, who was one of the high school hotties, had ended up in jail because of a cocaine habit. She had every right to be cautious of others.

The library was empty that early in the morning. Katie was grateful. She could finish her term paper without all the noise of people whispering. Jamie left and went to her first class. "See you at the end of the day, Katie!"

Katie finished her paper just as the first bell rang. She got up and looked around. There was no sign of any other students entering the library that morning, so there was no wait for the printer. Katie saved her work, printed it off, and headed up to turn in her completed work to her teacher. Ms. Philips was surprised to see her that morning.

"I thought you worked off school property in the mornings, Katie. I really didn't expect you to hand in your paper until next week. I'm glad you're finished. Gives me a jump on reading and grading your paper. And I'm sure you'll do well," she said to Katie.

"Thank you, Ms. Philips. I hope you like it."

Katie picked up her book bag and walked away. She went to her locker before leaving for the rest of the day. She looked down at the floor of her locker. There was a dead mouse on the bottom of her locker. She leaped back and screeched a little. David, one of her classmates, came running to her aid.

"What's all the squealing about?" he asked.

"Look what's at the bottom of my locker. You'd squeal too."

He looked inside her locker and saw nothing except a pair of gym shoes. He picked them up and showed them to Katie. "Yeah, I would squeal if my gym shoes looked like yours."

She looked in her locker, but nothing was there. She shook

her head. "I guess I'm seeing things." She turned and walked away.

Katie didn't feel like spending the rest of the day in school. Besides, her term paper was the last thing she had to finish before graduation. Seniors who had completed their requirements were allowed to leave the campus, so Katie left for the day. She drove home and pulled into the garage to hide her car in case one of the neighbors got too nosy. As she entered the house, Teddy came through the doggy door.

"Teddy, you scared me, boy! Do you want some breakfast?"

He started barking as if to answer her.

Katie went to the cupboard to get Teddy some food. A slew of cockroaches started climbing up her arms. She dropped the can of dog food and headed for the sink to brush them off her arms. When she leaned over, there were no cockroaches on her arms. *Okay, I'm sleep deprived.* Or, she thought, maybe the antibiotics were doing something funny to her mind. She opened the can of dog food and poured it into Teddy's bowl. As she bent down, she noticed the morning paper on the table. The front-page headline read, "Woman Incarcerated due to Child Endangerment." Realizing it was Tommy Sampson's mom, she read on.

> Kimberly Sampson, age forty-four, was taken into custody late Thursday night due to endangering the welfare of her child. Mrs. Sampson was cooking dinner on Thursday, and she claims Tommy, her son, was helping her, when a pot of hot water fell on him. That's what she claims.

Tommy gave CYS a statement at the hospital, telling them why his mother would
do such a thing. Investigation is pending.

The paper fell to the floor.

"Why do I hold possession of something that is supposed
to help other people, and I can't help this kid out?" she said out
loud.

Katie cleaned after lunch, then went upstairs to take a
shower. It was difficult to keep her finger from getting wet. She
had little rubber sleeves that went around her finger to keep it
dry. She got into the shower and started washing her hair. The
soap dropped out of her hand, and when she bent to pick it up,
it wasn't soap; it was a scorpion. She jumped back and started
screaming. Then her eyes came into focus, and she realized it
was soap and not any creature lurking around the shower. *I need
to stop this craziness. If I don't, I'm going to end up in the loony
bin next to my mother.* She knew she had a couple hours before
Nana got home, so she put on her sweat suit and sneakers and
went for a walk.

The streets were quiet. Of course, all the kids were in
school, and anyone who needed to be at work was already there.
She walked down James Street and around the block. Once she
got to Elm Street, she thought she would climb up Oak Street
Hill instead of walking back home. As she walked up the hill,
she heard a couple of dogs barking out in front of one of the
houses. Then she felt her papa's watch burn her arm. "Ouch!"
she said, speaking a little louder than she intended. She looked
at the name on the mailbox: Dieffenbach. That was Paula's last
name. *What kind of evil comes from that house?* She just stood

there staring at the Cape house, which was painted gray and had black shutters. The house didn't look all that bad. Except for the paint chipping, it appeared to be an okay-looking house. Just then, an elderly woman came out of the house to yell at her dogs.

"Butch! Rugger! Get inside, you mangy mutts!"

Katie waved to the woman, who just shrugged and walked inside. Katie turned around and started walking back down the hill. Papa's watch quit burning her arm after she was out of sight from the house on the hill. She walked faster toward home and saw Nana's car in the driveway. *Oh boy, I'm in trouble for parking in the garage.* She got to the front porch and immediately heard Teddy barking, announcing her arrival home. She opened the door to see Nana in her recliner, reading her Bible. Nana looked up at Katie over her reading glasses.

"Katie, I thought you'd be at school!"

"No, I got my term paper done, and the other classes I'm taking I have already passed. I wasn't feeling well, so I decided I'd come home."

"I didn't see your car," Nana said.

"I parked in the garage, hoping to keep the neighbors at bay." She grinned. "Nana, do you have a minute?"

Suddenly, the phone rang. It was Nana's friend Joyce. *I guess I'm not going to be able to talk to my grandmother for at least an hour.* Joyce never got off the phone quickly. Katie decided to go to her room and read while her grandmother was occupied by her friend. Teddy followed her upstairs. He liked being in Katie's bedroom. The afternoon sun rays came through the window, and Teddy liked sitting in the sun.

Katie heard Nana mumbling something to Joyce about

having her sweater somewhere around the house. Nana had borrowed Joyce's sweater the last time they went to bingo. Joyce had been having hot flashes and loaned the sweater to Nana. Katie remembered it because she thought the sweater was cute, a baby-blue button down. Of course, it wasn't anything her grandmother wore. She was always complaining about Joyce's choice in clothes. She said she always tried dressing younger than she should have. Katie had told Nana she looked good in the sweater. Of course, Nana had rolled her eyes and called her silly.

Katie lay down on her bed, reading a book, and found herself fast asleep. It was dark outside when she woke up. She went downstairs to find Nana. *Teddy must have gotten up and left my room before Nana left.* There was a note on the kitchen table.

> Katie, sorry I missed you tonight. Joyce asked me to come to her house for a few days to help her paint her living room. Dinner is in the microwave. If you need anything, call me. Love, Nana

I guess I won't get any answers from Nana again. She opened the microwave to get dinner. It was spaghetti. She loved Nana's spaghetti. She sat down and ate in silence. She thought about calling Jamie to come over, but she knew Jamie had to work on her term paper, so she decided she would eat and go to bed.

CHAPTER 8

~

BSU

Going back to work after being off for a few days was a little tiring. Katie felt she never had quite enough days off. However, she loved the job she was doing for the BSU. She knew she could potentially help more people in ways others could not.

She swiped her badge and entered the elevator. Suddenly, she felt her arm burn. She knew Paula must not be far away. The bell dinged, and the elevator opened. She was greeted by Cathy, one of the nurses. Cathy was a beautiful redhead with crystal-blue eyes. She had lost her husband to cancer a few years back and thought she would never find happiness again. However, when an intern from Australia came to work at the BSU, Cathy found out that love did exist after death.

Cathy informed Katie that Paula was in rare form that day. She said Katie needed to tread lightly. "She had a fit last night and started throwing chairs at staff and screaming like a wild child. They had to sedate her. So, she's calmer today and a little annoyed at the world."

Katie told her she would put her jacket away and see if she could get anything out of her that day. She swiped her badge to the breakroom and entered. As she opened her locker, she was startled by a dead mouse on the locker floor. She looked twice to make sure it was there before she got ahold of maintenance. She walked out of the breakroom to let Cathy know of the little visitor in her locker and see if she could get ahold of Tim, the maintenance man. Cathy said he'd just left for a cup of coffee, but she would try his radio. Katie asked if she could put her coat and purse in Cathy's office. Cathy took her things, and Katie went off to the children's ward. The first person she ran into was Georgia. She was rocking in a chair in the corner.

"Hey, Georgia, how are you doing?"

She looked up and smiled. "I'm doing really good. I get to go home today, Katie."

"Do you want to talk about anything while I'm here?"

"Yes, but could we go in my room? I would feel more comfortable."

Katie followed her to her room. It was small, with a twin bed on either side of the room. There were a desk and a chair in the corner of the room and a bathroom in the corner on the other side. Katie pulled up a chair, and they started talking.

"Katie, I really am doing a lot better. The staff has been very helpful. I can't deny the pills they are giving me help as well. But I have decided what I want to do. I'm going to try to work with the staff in weekly counseling sessions and eventually get off the medication."

"That sounds great, Georgia!"

"Yes, and I think I'm going to join the military. I spoke to a counselor, James, who was in the military, and he is going to help me. I have to be off the medication for two years before they will let me join, but then I can see the world and take Jeremy with me."

Katie raised her eyebrows in question.

"Not in a literal sense. But Jeremy will always be with me."

"I am so happy for you. You really have come to realize that death is a part of life. What we experience in our lives makes up who we are today. It really sounds awesome, Sweetie!"

"It was James who helped me through this all. He lost his best friend to a car accident when he was sixteen. They had plans to go to school at the same college. So, you can imagine how close they were. He helped me understand that life doesn't end when we lose someone. We have to take control of our own destiny."

Papa's watch didn't move. *I guess that's a good sign.* "Well, Georgia, I have to talk with the other kids on the floor. I will probably run into you during one of your counseling sessions with James. Again, I am so happy for you!"

Katie went into the TV lounge and looked around. Paula wasn't anywhere. She checked her bedroom, and Paula appeared to be asleep. It was a big relief. Katie wasn't sure if she was ready to take her on that day. Back in the TV lounge a young man was putting a puzzle together. Katie approached him cautiously for fear she would startle him. He appeared to be concentrating hard on the pieces of the puzzle.

"Hi. I'm Katie. What's your name?"

He never took his eyes off the puzzle. "Tobin," he said grumpily.

"Hi, Tobin. Do you want to talk with me today?"

"Does it look like I want to talk with anyone? Now, if you have a cigarette, I wouldn't mind smoking it. You got one?" He looked up at her in a devilish manner.

"Sorry. I can't help you out, buddy. Maybe you'll want to talk to me another day?"

"Maybe," he said, going back to his puzzle.

Looking around, Katie saw a young girl fidgeting with her shirttail. She walked over and introduced herself. "Hi. I'm Katie. What's your name?"

The girl looked up, wide-eyed, and said softly, "Tessa."

"Would you like to talk with me today?"

"What for? No one bothers listening to me anyway."

"That's my job here, Tessa. It's to listen when you're talking. If you have a problem, we can try to work it out together. We could talk out here in the lounge, or we could go into your room," Katie said, looking for any sign of a conversation.

"I would like to go into my room, but my roommate is sleeping," she said, a little annoyed.

"I can ask staff if we can use one of their offices. Would you like that?"

Tessa nodded, and Katie went to the nurses' station to find Cathy.

"Hey Cathy, would you have an office available for me to speak with a client? Tessa would like to talk to me, but her roommate is sleeping."

"I don't know how you do it, Katie; we have been trying to get her to talk to us since she got here last night," Cathy said, shaking her head.

"She probably wasn't ready."

"C'mon, Katie. Give yourself some credit. You have a way with these kids that I have never seen before. I have been here for five years, and you're the first person to get a child to talk to you when asked. Let me check Dr. Faulk's office. I'm pretty sure it's empty. He's in meetings all morning."

Cathy went to check the office while Katie sat there waiting. All the doors had rectangular windows on them, so a person could peek into an office without disturbing a patient.

"You can use Dr. Faulk's office."

"Thanks, Cathy!"

Katie went back into the TV lounge to find Tessa. She wasn't in the lounge, so Katie went to her room. Papa's watch started burning her arm. She knew immediately that Paula was awake. She waited in the lounge outside Tessa's room, waiting for her to come out, thinking she must have gone into the bathroom. Paula came peeking out of her room and gave Katie a stare that sent chills up her spine.

"Oh, you're here again? I was sure you weren't coming back after that tragic accident with your finger," Paula said in a snarky tone.

"I just needed a couple days off to recuperate. I'm back now."

Katie thought, *how did she know about my finger? Someone must have mentioned it, and she overheard the conversation.* That was her theory, and she was sticking to it.

"I don't know why you want to talk to Ms. Fancy Pants. She hasn't said a word to anyone since arriving here."

"Paula, I don't think that is any of your concern." Papa's watched started to really heat up her arm.

"What's your title here anyway?" Paula asked in a loud voice.

"I am a medical advocate."

"Oh, so really, you're a nobody, and you don't have any authority over anything or anyone here?"

"Well, I do answer to my boss, but I'm here in hopes that if you need my assistance with anything outside of the BSU, I can help in some way. My input during our meetings goes back to my boss, and we figure out the best way we can help once you're released from here," Katie said.

"So, when are you going to have time for me?"

"I can speak to you right after I get finished with Tessa if you like."

"That won't be necessary. I think she is tied up. I think you'll have time now."

"Let me check on her, and I will let you know," Katie said as she walked away from Paula and into the bedroom.

She heard Tessa in the bathroom, violently vomiting. She knocked on the door. "Tessa, are you okay in there? Do you want me to get someone?" Katie said to her, shaking a little, thinking, *what has Paula done?*

She yelled back through the door, "Yes, please!"

Katie walked to the nurses' station to see if she could find one of them. The new staff member sitting at the desk was eager to help. Katie told her what was happening with Tessa. She told Katie she would have to leave the unit that day. "The flu bug is going around, and unless you're a registered nurse, you have to leave the building."

Katie told her she would be fine. "I got the flu shot before I started working here."

The nurse informed Katie it was protocol. "You should call back in the morning to see if anything changes."

Katie told her she needed to get her briefcase, which she'd left in the TV lounge. She said she would get it for Katie. Katie then introduced herself.

"By the way, I'm Katie O'Reilly. I work for the Victims' Advocacy Center. I'm their medical advocate."

She shook Katie's hand and said her name was Raymie. She was there temporarily as a traveling nurse from Rochester, New York. She grabbed Katie's briefcase from the lounge and handed it to her. "Remember to call in the morning. We should know about six thirty if it's clear to come back in to work."

Katie went to get her coat from the breakroom but remembered Cathy had put it in her office, so she waited until Raymie got back from Tessa's room to ask her for it. As Katie sat there, Paula peeked her head around the corner and gave her a devilish grin. Katie had to wonder if she'd had anything to do with the sudden outbreak. Then she thought that was a bunch of nonsense. *How could anyone, unless she was sick, bring about the flu? Katie, you're overthinking.* However, the watch burned her arm when Paula looked at her.

Raymie came out of the children's ward. "I thought you were leaving, Ms. O'Reilly," Raymie said with some authority.

"Please call me Katie. I am leaving as soon as I collect my coat from Cathy's office."

"Oh, well, let me get that for you."

Katie took her coat and headed for the elevator. She swiped her badge to go downstairs. Leaving the elevator, she spotted Tammy. She worked at registration. Tammy was a sweetie. She had made Katie feel right at home when she first arrived there. They talked sometimes when Katie was not in a hurry and Tammy was not busy.

"Hi, Tammy. How are you doing?"

"I'm good. What are you doing down here so early? Did one of the kids attack anyone today?"

"No, a flu virus broke out, and they shut the ward down for the rest of the day. The only people who can be on the floor are the patients and the nurses," Katie said, a little disappointed.

"I heard something about it. Seems like it came about overnight. Only a couple kids caught it," Tammy said with a funny face.

"Do you know which kids?"

"I'm not sure. Why do you ask?" Tammy said with her eyebrows raised.

"Do you know anything about the young girl they brought in on Thursday? The one with the dark hair and even darker eyes?" Papa's watch started getting warm on her arm.

"You mean the one with the star tattoo on her hand? I don't know much about her other than she gave me the creeps. When I was checking her into the system, I got a chill down my spine. It felt weird. I have never felt that way about a child before." She looked disturbed.

"I'm not sure what her story is, but it seems like every time I get a chance to speak to her, something happens, and we end up not talking. It's probably just a coincidence. I guess I'll have to wait until tomorrow. Well, Tammy, I'm going to get out of here. I will see you tomorrow."

"Bye, Katie. Have a good day!"

It wasn't lunchtime yet. Katie thought about calling Jamie. *Maybe we could meet for lunch today. She would be in study hall right now, and she could answer my text.* She pulled her cell phone out of her purse and shot Jamie a text. Jamie responded faster than Katie had thought she would.

"Katie, I'm as sick as a dog. The flu bug hit. Talk to you later!"

Here I was, thinking Paula had something to do with the illness going around. I'm losing my mind!

Just as Katie was getting into her car, she looked up and saw Paula. Paula was looking at her and laughing. *What an odd girl.* She still sent a chill through Katie. Papa's watch was warm on her arm. She fumbled with the keys to get into her car. Instead of unlocking the car, she set off the alarm. She hurried to shut it off before security came out the door. She finally got into her car and let out a big sigh. What was her deal? Why did Papa's watch warn her every time that girl was around? She started her car and drove home.

Nana's car was in the driveway. She was excited to see that Nana was home. *Finally, I might get a chance to speak to her.* As Katie started to get out of her car, her phone pinged. It was her grandmother, letting her know she would not be home that night. She had gone out with some friends, and she said dinner was in the microwave and not to wait up for her. Katie was disappointed once again. She knew that when Nana went out with her friends, she wouldn't be home until the next day. She always fell asleep on Joyce's couch while watching movies.

Every time I feel as if I'm going to be able to talk to her, it always gets interrupted by something or someone. Katie thought it was odd that Nana had left so soon. It wasn't even lunchtime yet. Teddy greeted Katie at the door. He was her one constant, always there when she needed him.

She popped open the microwave, but nothing was in it.

Nana must have forgotten to put in dinner. She opened the fridge and found some chili, so she heated it up for lunch. She took off her coat and hung it in the closet. She went to grab her slippers, and Teddy started growling at something outside. Two girls were walking by. She told Teddy to be quiet. *I guess he just wanted to let me know they were there.*

She went back into the kitchen and opened the cupboard to grab some crackers. She jumped back and screamed—another dead mouse. She went to retrieve the dustpan and get some cleaning supplies from under the sink. When she got back to the cupboard, the mouse was gone. *What is going on? Why am I seeing things that aren't there? I need some sleep. Maybe the medication for my finger is messing with my mind.* Then she remembered the mouse at work. *I need to mention something to Cathy. I will ask her if Tim cleaned it up.* She put the dustpan back into the cupboard, put away the cleaning supplies, and sat down to eat her chili. She saw something move in her bowl and spooned it out. There was a worm in her chili. *Where in the hell did it come from?* She threw the bowl into the sink and ran water to help the food go down the garbage disposal. *There goes my appetite.*

She went into the living room to watch some TV. She needed to get her mind off what had been going on around her. She flipped through the channels and settled on watching ID. *They always get the bad guys. I need something positive.* Investigative Discovery was probably not the greatest pick, especially due to the heinous crimes that were committed. But they did catch the bad guys.

When Katie woke up, it was dark outside. She couldn't understand why she kept falling asleep and for so long. *I haven't been exercising lately. Or taking my walks.* Nana wasn't going to be home that night, and she was hungry. Her stomach started growling. She went to the kitchen to find something simple to eat and settled on a bowl of cereal. That would be quick and easy. She poured herself a bowl of Raisin Bran, hoping no creatures came out of the box. She opened the fridge and grabbed the milk.

"Crap!" The milk had expired a couple days ago. She poured the milk down the sink with the chunks that followed. *I guess I'm not supposed to eat today.* She put the Raisin Bran back in the box. She was hungry, so she decided on toast. *You can't go wrong with bread and butter.* She put the bread in the toaster and quickly ran to the bathroom. When she came out, she smelled something burning. "Ugh!" It was her toast. She grabbed it, and of course, it was burned. It hurt her hand, so she dropped the piece of bread onto the ground. Before she knew what was happening, Teddy scarfed it up. She had one piece left to eat. She scraped most of the burned parts into the garbage and settled on the one piece of toast she was going to eat that night.

It was about ten thirty, and Katie headed for bed. She climbed the steps one at a time, thinking about all she'd been through in the last few weeks. This new journey in life she was on was taking its toll on her body. She got up to her room with Teddy following right behind. He looked at her as if she'd forgotten something. She had. He needed to be let out for the night to go potty. Back down the stairs they went. At night, Teddy wouldn't use the doggy door. They had to let him outside by opening the back door. She let him out to do his business and waited for five minutes. He finally came back inside, and they both headed to bed.

The sun was coming up over the light pole and shining

brightly into Katie's bedroom. She felt refreshed after a good night's sleep. She'd had no bad dreams that she could remember. She went into the bathroom to brush her teeth. When she came back out, she realized she needed to call the BSU to see if she could go in to work that day. The phone rang a couple times. When someone picked up on the other end, she knew immediately it was Cathy.

"Hey, Cathy, it's Katie. Is the coast clear, or do I have to take another day off?"

"Hi, Katie! No, you can come back in today. I think it was just a twenty-four-hour thing. No one else has come up sick. By the time night medications were given, the kids seemed fine. By the way, Paula wants to talk to you this morning. She seems excited. Can you come in a little earlier?"

"Sure, I will be in as soon as I grab a shower."

She thought it was odd that Cathy had said Paula seemed excited. *She was anything but excited to see me.* She noticed her arm wasn't burning. Despite saying Paula's name, nothing happened.

Katie hurried with her shower, got dressed fast, and headed out the door. She jumped into her car, waiting for Papa's watch to start burning her arm, but it didn't. She arrived at the BSU twenty minutes later, walked into the building, and greeted Tammy. Katie swiped her badge, and up the elevator she went. Paula was in the doorway to the elevator when she got upstairs, and she greeted Katie. She looked great. Her hair was nice and clean and out of her face. She had color in her cheeks. Even her eyes looked brighter.

"Good morning, Katie!"

"Good morning, Paula. It's nice to see you this morning."

She meant it. There was something different about Paula. Papa's watch wasn't warning her off either.

"I'm ready to talk to you, Katie. I know you are the only one who can help me. You and Dr. Faulk," Paula said with a big grin on her face.

"Where would you like to talk, Paula?"

"Cathy is holding Dr. Faulk's office for us. He has meetings all morning long, so no one will interrupt us," she said, grabbing Katie's arm and pulling her toward Dr. Faulk's office. "He is a very nice man!"

"Yes, I'm aware of Dr. Faulk, Paula. I know he's a very nice man," Katie said.

"Hurry, Katie. We don't have much time!"

They entered the office and sat down. Paula looked up at Katie and started talking.

"Okay, Katie, do you want to know what's going on with me? I hope I don't get interrupted," Paula said with a shaky voice.

"Don't worry; we won't get interrupted. They know not to bother us when I'm with a client."

"You don't understand, Katie. I'm not worried about them. I'm worried about Priscilla." She looked a little scared.

"Is Priscilla a new girl on the ward?"

"No, Katie, you don't understand!" she said a little louder.

"I'm trying to understand, Paula. Explain what you mean, sweetie."

Suddenly, Paula's head went into her lap. When she raised her head, she looked different. Papa's watch started burning Katie's arm. She forced herself to look at Paula. Her eyes were darker. Katie's heart started beating so hard and fast that she wondered if Paula could hear it. A moment of silence passed. Katie looked up at the ceiling as if the wall were going to come down on her; that was how heavy the air felt. She finally got up the nerve to say something. Her voice was low and hoarse. She was startled by her own voice.

"Hi, Priscilla. Do you want to talk to me?"

I knew whom Paula had been talking about as soon as she looked up at me. Paula was a sweet, innocent girl. Priscilla was a different kind of girl.

"Priscilla would be correct. At last someone with some brain activity. I knew if anyone was going to figure it out, it would be you, Katie. Dr. Faulk was getting close. Especially on days when I was very tired. Paula would open her big mouth and try to tell him. Now that you know, are you going to be like her insensitive grandmother and try to get rid of me? Because if you do, you'll wish you'd never met me!"

"Can I ask you something, Priscilla?" Katie's eyes darted left and then right and landed on the plastic cup she had in her hand. Her skin felt as if needles were being pricked into her body. "When did you first appear in Paula's life?"

Just as Priscilla was going to say something, there was a knock at the door.

Katie had to remind herself to breathe. "Come in!"

It was Dr. Faulk.

"I'm sorry, Doctor. This was the only office available. We will get our stuff and leave." Katie started to collect her stuff.

"No, don't be silly. I just need to grab some papers near my computer." He looked at Paula. "Take your time, Katie. I will talk to you soon." He looked back as he shut the door. He nodded and walked off.

"You know, he's a typical man. A little awkward at times and difficult to read. People around here treat him like a celebrity and not like a doctor should be treated," Priscilla said with a smirk on her face.

"How do you think a doctor should be treated, Paula?"

"Excuse me! It's Priscilla!"

"I'm so sorry, Priscilla. Are you going to answer my question?"

"Well, isn't it obvious? They treat him like he's one of their friends. Clearly, he needs to be respected a little more than that," Priscilla said with a nasty tone.

"Doctors are human too, Priscilla." Katie had to keep saying her name out loud. She would have called her Paula. "So, Priscilla, can you explain to me how you came into Paula's life?"

"Why should I tell you? You know more than most people know. Even her idiot grandmother isn't smart enough to figure it out. She just wants to get rid of us. She's the one who put us here. If it hadn't been for her, I would have never shown up."

"Why are you blaming her grandmother?" Katie asked in a softer voice.

"You fool, I'm not saying she was to blame. I'm saying it's her fault I arrived."

"Okay, now I am not following you."

"She didn't do anything except go to work. It was her stupid boyfriend who created us. If she hadn't invited him to live with us, this would have never happened. If I could shoot someone and get away with it, I would shoot Pete right between his eyes!" Priscilla said with a disgusted look on her face.

"Why don't you tell me what happened—from the beginning?" Katie asked.

"It all started last Friday night. My grandmother got called into work, and Pete took me to his restaurant for dinner. Everything was going so nice. He seemed like he was interested in my life and my friends. We had a great time at dinner. He even told me he was going to ask my grandmother to marry him. Blah, blah, blah. It was when we got home that his whole demeanor changed. I found out what his true intentions were about. He pushed me up against the refrigerator and told me I owed him for dinner. He started taking my shirt off. I asked him to stop. I told him Grandma would be home soon. He informed me she wasn't going to be home that night; she was covering the shift of a girl who'd called in sick. I scratched his arm and tried pushing him away from me. He's a lot bigger than I am and got the better of me. He raped me in the kitchen. I vomited after he was done. He said thanks and walked out of the house. When Paula's grandma came home, she blamed her for sending him away. She tried calling him and texting him, but he refused to take her calls. I couldn't believe her grandmother wouldn't listen. The pain was so deep. That's when I showed up. Paula tried killing herself, and that's when we got put in here. That girl doesn't listen to me. I told her we could get him good." Priscilla took a deep breath.

"What did your grandma do when you told her?"

"She wouldn't believe me. She called me a liar. I wanted to protect Paula. That's when I showed up. Paula wishes she could take that whole night back."

Just then, Papa's watch started spinning. The hourglass turned upside down. Paula was back at her grandmother's house. Katie was out walking Teddy and ran into her. Paula walked over to her and gave her a big hug.

"She's gone! She's really gone. Priscilla is not here, and I'm going to stay at my girlfriend's house tonight. I am going to live with my father as soon as I can. I won't be left alone with Pete. Thank you for everything, Katie. You saved my life!"

She walked to her house, waved, and smiled. Katie felt happy for her. *Things do work out for the best.* Katie walked toward home and felt good for the first time in a while. Teddy started pulling on his chain. He was hungry, and she was too. She ran to the front porch with Teddy pulling her. She had to hurry up and eat and change. She had to get back to the BSU. She wanted to see if Tessa was available to talk. Hopefully she was feeling better, and they could talk. Katie grabbed a quick sandwich and went out the door.

CHAPTER 9

Tessa

By the time Katie got back to the BSU, the kids were finishing lunch. She knew she had helped Paula as much as she could for now. She wanted to talk to Tessa. Tammy wasn't at registration, so Katie swiped her badge and entered the elevator to go up. *Ping.* She was on the second floor. Raymie was the first person she ran into. Raymie looked as if she had just come from the gym. Her hair was askew, and sweat rolled down both sides of her face. Even her mascara was running down her face.

"Raymie, what's going on?" Katie asked, not sure if she really wanted to know.

"The bell rang to announce lunch for the kids, and when I went into the TV lounge to get Tobin, he started throwing chairs and cursing at everyone. He started calling me names I have never heard come out of an adult's mouth, let alone a child's. I interrupted him while he was doing his puzzle, and he went from a Dr. Jekyll to a Mr. Hyde personality. It took two guards to strap him down. You know that kid is small, but he had the strength of a grown man. Very violent also," Raymie said, out of breath.

"What's his story, Raymie?" Katie asked.

"Dr. Faulk isn't certain yet. I do know he's having a family counseling session tonight. Well, at least with his dad. His mother died a month ago, and he has become quite a handful. I guess I can't blame him. I'm not sure how I would feel if I lost my mom," Raymie said with her head down.

"Yeah, unfortunate things happen all the time; you just never know. Is Tessa feeling okay? I would like to talk to her."

She gave Katie a funny look. "She is feeling okay. She's in her room. Why do you ask?" Raymie said, looking at Katie as if she had two heads.

"I thought she got the flu bug that was going around," Katie said not thinking about having been at the BSU earlier because of the watch.

"Oh, is that why you're late, you thought she was sick?" Raymie asked, looking at her.

"No, I had to run by the school to submit my term paper for graduation," Katie lied.

"The last time I saw Tessa, she was in her room. You can go in if you'd like," Raymie said, walking away

"Thank you, Raymie!"

Katie headed for Tessa's room. She was in the TV lounge when she entered. "Hey, Tessa, how are you doing today?"

She was a fragile girl. She had beautiful brown hair and big brown eyes. She appeared a lot younger than she was. She said she had been waiting for Katie all morning. Katie apologized and asked if she wanted to talk to her now. Tessa asked if they could go into her room to talk. She was afraid of Tobin coming back out and causing a scene. She got up, and they both walked to her room.

"Are you sure you're here to help me?"

Katie assured her that was her job to try to help the kids on that floor.

"Are you Catholic?" Tessa asked.

"I was baptized Catholic and grew up Catholic, but I haven't been a very good one. I have been missing Mass quite a bit lately."

"Do you know Father Ron?" Tessa asked.

"Yes, I know him."

Tessa looked at the floor. "Did you know he's in love with me?"

Katie's eyes opened wide. "Wait—what? Tessa, he's a priest!"

Tessa looked up at Katie. "No one believes me. My mother said it was blasphemy. She said it was sacrilegious to think that way about a priest. Sister Ann doesn't believe me. Neither does Deacon Mark. They all say I'm crazy and under some demonic spell. Katie, I'm not going crazy! Please don't think less of me for what I'm about to tell you."

"I'm here to listen, not to judge."

Tessa cleared her throat. "Well, it started out with me helping out with Sunday school. Then he would ask me to stay and clean the erasers with him. It seemed like we were there for hours. My friend Michele told me we were only cleaning them for like fifteen minutes. I'm telling you, Katie, it seemed a lot longer. He also treated me older than I am. I will be seventeen next month. He also asked me if I had a boyfriend. I told him

I have a boy who is a friend of mine, but he's not my boyfriend. He would question me about Peter all the time. I kept telling him he was just a friend of mine. That's when Father Ron started texting me. He kept asking me to help him with Sunday school and cleaning the church. He asked me out.

"Our first meeting was at the doughnut shop down the street. We had hot chocolate together. I will never forget. It was a cold day in April. The hot chocolate made me feel warm inside. That's when he asked me to start coming to the rectory to help with some cleaning. Of course, I was happy to help. He is a hunk. When he started showing more feelings toward me, I started getting a little creeped out. After all, he's a man of God. I would say to myself, 'Father Ron is not interested in you, Tessa. You're just imagining things.' I always felt that he looked at me like I was someone special.

"Our next encounter was when he invited me to dinner. We were finished cleaning the rectory, and he said he wanted to celebrate. So, I met him. I even told my mom that he invited me to dinner for all the work I have been helping him with and said we were going to celebrate. She gave me her blessing, and off I went. It was six thirty, and Father had asked me to meet him at six forty-five. Of course, I was going to be punctual. A little too punctual. Father Ron was sitting at the corner table when I got there. He had ordered an appetizer and a copper-colored drink. I was pretty sure it was alcohol. I brushed past him, and I felt as if my skin were on fire. He asked me if I wanted something to drink. I ordered a Diet Coke. The waitress came and took our order. He was looking at me. Like really looking at me. I was blushing under the light. I was sure he wanted to kiss me. I am sure he felt the same way I did. Oh my God, Katie, the next thing that happened was he lifted his glass and toasted to us finishing the cleaning at the rectory.

"I'm an idiot, Katie! He didn't love me. I just realized in talking to you that he was just being nice. I'm the one who is in love with my priest. Why didn't I see it until now? Maybe I did. Maybe that's why I took all those pills. I knew he didn't really love me, yet I dreamed this all up. Katie, he's being moved because of me. They're sending him to another parish. What have I done, Katie?"

"You're young, and you now realize your feelings for your priest are one-sided."

"Katie, what am I going to do? I just ruined a priest. They're moving him because of me. What am I going to do? If I could take everything back, I would."

Just then, Papa's watch started spinning, and the hourglass turned upside down. Tessa was outside the rectory, when Katie walked by with Jamie. Tessa looked up and mouthed, "Thank you!" Katie nodded and walked along with Jamie.

"Do you know that girl?" Jamie asked.

Katie told her, "She goes to my church, and I loaned her money for collections one time."

Tessa knew she had been taken back in time. Father Ron would be safe. She knew his intentions were pure. She had a do-over.

Jamie and Katie finished their walk, and Katie had to get back to the BSU. She waved goodbye, got into her car, and drove back to the BSU.

CHAPTER 10

Tobin

Tobin was sitting by himself when Katie entered the TV lounge. He was coughing and sneezing. She asked him if he was ready to talk to her. He told her Cathy had just gone to get him his medicine. As soon as she got back and he took his medicine, he would be ready to talk.

"I'm guessing you don't want a cigarette," Katie said.

"No, I was just trying to be cool. A lot of the kids at school smoke. Especially after school and, I hear, at parties. I guess they think it makes them look more grown up. Besides, I can't stand cigarettes. I have asthma." He spoke while looking at his puzzle.

Cathy came into the lounge with his medicine. Katie asked Tobin where he wanted to talk. He said they could talk there in the TV lounge.

"So, Tobin, why don't you tell me a little bit about yourself?"

Tobin started speaking with his head down. "I just lost my

mom. She was in a car accident. She had been sick for quite some time. She always got sick after she ate."

"Did she have stomach problems?" Katie asked.

"No, she had weight problems. She never wanted to get fat."

"Oh, I see." *She must have been bulimic or anorexic*, Katie thought.

"My father buries himself in his work. Then there's my brother, J.T. He never has time for me. His life revolves around his friends and football. I don't really have anyone now that my mother is gone. She was my world. The day she died; she was leaving the hospital after seeing my brother. He got hurt at school. Him and another guy got into a fight, and J.T. got hurt bad. I didn't want to live after my mom died. Dad looks at me in a disgusted way, like I have done something to him. Like he is disappointed that I am his son."

"Tobin, you can't believe that. I'm sure your dad loves you. He is going through a lot right now; give him some time. I'm sure he's missing your mom also."

"I don't want to live anymore!" Tobin yelled.

Katie wasn't sure what to do. Just then, Cathy came in to check on them.

"Is everything okay in here?"

"I'm okay, Cathy. I was just talking to Katie. I will keep it down." Tobin was staring at the floor. He started backing up and mumbling something.

"What did you say?" Katie asked.

"I wasn't talking to you! Where is my dad? Why doesn't he want to see me?" Tobin stared into the corner as if someone were there talking to him.

"Tobin, I'm over here," said Katie.

Tobin wouldn't take his eyes off the corner.

"What do you say I have a talk with Dr. Faulk and ask him to get your father in here tonight? Your father and your brother. You could have a family meeting."

"Sure, whatever you think is good," replied Tobin.

Katie was waiting for Papa's watch to move, but nothing happened. Katie thought, *I guess this one needs to be fixed on its own.* She got up and walked out to the nurses' station. She asked Cathy if Dr. Faulk was available.

"Let me check, Katie. I think you might be in luck."

Cathy came back and said that Dr. Faulk would see me. Katie opened his door and sat down.

"Hi, Katie. How's it going with Tobin?"

"I'm a little confused by his outbursts and his mumbling. It's almost as if he is talking to someone else, when I'm clearly the only one in the room," Katie said.

"You would be correct, Katie. He is speaking with someone else. Tobin has schizophrenia. He has been diagnosed with paranoid schizophrenia. It's a chronic mental disorder in which an individual loses touch with reality. Tobin is being transferred in the morning. He will be placed in a clinic that studies these symptoms and is able to help people in ways we aren't capable of. Early intervention is the best chance of a positive outcome. I've spoken with his father. He agrees that Tobin needs this additional help. He was probably showing kindness to you, but I can tell you he is very violent. The death of his mother triggered the onset of his disease. He thought you could help him get out of this situation. He knows he's leaving tomorrow," said Dr. Faulk.

"That's why he asked me to set up a meeting with his dad and brother tonight," said Katie.

"Last night was unbearable. He was hearing voices, and they were telling him to kill Raymie. That's why he was in the TV lounge by himself. We can't trust him around anybody. If it wasn't for the fact that he specifically asked to speak with you, you wouldn't have been allowed in the room with him. Also, he was just given his medication. That has calmed him down immensely."

"Thank you, Doctor. That explains a lot to me. I had an inkling he had a disorder, but I wasn't sure. What am I going to tell Tobin then? He asked me to set up a meeting with his dad."

"Don't worry about Tobin. He will be out soon. The medication he is on makes him very tired. He will be asleep shortly."

"Again, thank you, Doctor. Oh, and good luck with Tobin."

"Thank you, Katie. The ward is quiet today. Why don't you take the rest of the day off? I'm sure you probably have work for school to do. I will see you in the morning."

As Katie walked to the breakroom, they were bringing another young girl into the BSU. Katie wouldn't be able to speak with her that day anyway. The girl had to meet with James and do an intake, and then they would decide if they should admit her.

Katie swiped her badge and entered the breakroom. To her surprise, Tobin was sitting at the table. He kept his eyes on the floor and said, "Katie, I'm very disappointed in you. You said you would help me!" He was angry.

"Tobin, I just got out of Dr. Faulk's office. He said you were going to have a meeting tonight." She lied, but she didn't want to upset him anymore.

He started walking backward. He was mumbling something. It gave Katie the chance to open the door and run out.

"Code red in the breakroom! Code red in the breakroom!" she screamed.

Two guards appeared out of nowhere. Katie pointed to the breakroom. "He's in there."

The guards opened the door. No one was inside. Katie looked and didn't see Tobin. "Where did he go? He was just in there."

"Who's *he*, miss?"

"The young boy—Tobin."

"Miss, you know no one is allowed in the breakroom without authorization. Plus, you have to have a badge to open the door."

Just then, Cathy walked out of the children's ward. "Kat, what's going on here?"

"Cathy, Tobin was just in the breakroom!"

"Katie, if Tobin was in the breakroom, he must have a twin brother. I just checked on him, and he's sound asleep in his room. You were in the lounge when I gave him his medication. It didn't take him long to go down."

"Wow, I must be tired, Cathy."

"Why don't you go home and get some rest? We have one intake, and Tobin is being transferred in the morning."

"Yeah, I guess I have been burning the candle at both ends. I will take your advice and get out of here. Oh, before I go, did Tim say anything about that mouse in my locker?"

"No, he never mentioned it."

"Okay, thanks, Cathy. I will see you tomorrow."

Katie grabbed her stuff out of her locker and headed for the elevator. She swiped her badge and pushed the ground-floor button. She was happy to see that Tammy wasn't at her desk. She just needed to get home.

Katie drove slowly, not wanting to talk to anyone that day. She pulled into the driveway. Nana was at work, so she could go into the house without conversation. Teddy was barking when she walked onto the porch. He was at the front door to greet Katie when she walked into the living room. She took her coat off and hung it up in the closet. She walked up the stairs with Teddy following close behind. She threw her briefcase onto her desk and lay down with her clothes on. Sleep came quickly. She didn't remember her head hitting the pillow.

This time, she wasn't as lucky. As soon as she closed her eyes, the dream came alive. Tobin was standing in front of her. Edith, Paula, Tessa, and Georgia were all standing behind him. They were all chanting, "She's a fake. She's a fake."

Katie tried running, but her feet wouldn't move. They all came closer and closer. Teddy started growling, and they backed away.

Katie woke up from the dream and found Teddy growling at something in her closet. She slowly opened the door. There wasn't anything inside.

"What's going on, boy? What are you growling at?" She sat down and started petting him. "You're such a good boy; you're just protecting me. I love you, Teddy."

Katie started crying for no reason. She went back to her bed and pulled her cell phone from her purse. She thought she would shoot Jamie a text, hoping she would be up for dinner or something. Jamie texted right back.

"Sorry, Katie. I'm buried in work right now. Maybe we could do dinner another night?"

She knew Nana wasn't due home until later, so she went to the kitchen and started dinner. She would make her famous meatloaf. She got out some hamburger and put it in the microwave to defrost the meat. Just then, the phone rang. Katie looked at the caller ID. It was the BSU. She picked up the phone and immediately knew the voice on the other end of the line.

"Hi, Cathy. What's up?"

"Katie, I know you were going to take the rest of the day off, but I really need you here right now. We have a young girl who has been raped, and I need a counselor. Can you please come in and talk with her?"

"Let me get a quick shower, and I'll be there."

"You're a lifesaver. I will see you soon."

CHAPTER 11

Monya

Katie took a shower and forgot all about the hamburger in the microwave. She drove to the BSU. When she got there, Tammy was sitting at the front desk. They exchanged pleasantries, and then Katie went up to the second floor. Tammy had let her know they had two more intakes. *Looks like it's going to be a busy night*, Katie thought as the elevator pinged. As soon as she stepped off the elevator, Tobin was there to greet her.

"Hi, Tobin. How are you tonight?"

He spit at her and yelled, "Traitor!"

Cathy came out of the lounge and took Tobin to his room. She came back out and kept thanking Katie for coming in that night. She led Katie to the main office. Katie thought, *this must be a special case; we usually talk in the breakroom.*

"Okay, Katie, you need to sit down for this one. The media is involved, so you might want to tread lightly."

Katie couldn't imagine what would have brought the media to the BSU, but she sat there quietly and listened.

"Her name is Monya Sanchez. She's claiming Tony Sampson raped her. She came in pretty cut up. She said the only reason she was so cut up was because she wanted to get her brother's attention. Her brother Michael was going to kill Tony. So, I'm guessing she cut herself pretty good to make a statement and save her brother. Now you kind of understand why this case is so sensitive. Especially when the Sampson name is involved. I guess her brother and Tony were good friends. Tony was staying overnight at the Sanchez's house when it happened. Of course, H.G. is spewing all over the media that his son and Monya were lovers. He doesn't want his football star going to jail."

"Okay, I see what's happening here. Monya cut herself to save face. Also, to save her brother from jail time. So, I'm thinking it happened, and Tony, the little shit, is claiming it was consensual," Katie said.

"Exactly."

"Okay, let me put my coat away, and I will talk with her."

Katie walked to the breakroom, swiped her badge, and opened her locker, half expecting to see a mouse. She needed to ask Tim about it. *Maybe I will catch him tonight. I know he works the night shift sometimes.* She walked out of the breakroom and followed Cathy to the children's ward.

"She's in her room. Go on in; she is expecting you. I must talk to KTTC. The news station wants a comment. Of course, we have no comments. I don't know how they found out she was here. If you need anything, Katie, I will be out here." She pointed to the nurses' station.

Katie walked up to Monya's room and knocked on the door. No one answered, so she opened the door. Monya was sitting at the desk, staring at the wall. She was a pretty girl with long, curly black hair. She had the most beautiful greenish-brown eyes Katie had ever seen. She looked up as Katie walked closer to her.

"Hi, Monya. My name is Katie. I'm here to help you."

She looked as if she had been through a war zone. She had bandages up and down her arms. She didn't say anything. She just stared at Katie.

"I know what you're going through. I was sexually assaulted at your age," said Katie.

"I'm sure you have no idea what I'm going through. Did you have TV and newspapers in your face when it happened to you?"

"No, I didn't, but it was in the newspaper. By my testifying against my attacker, I put him away for ten years."

Katie remembered the day the DA had told her that if she didn't put him away, he would do it again. He had been on parole as it was, and her testimony had put him away for longer than just a parole violation.

Monya looked up at her. "I'm sorry. I didn't mean to make light of your situation." She was crying. "How am I going to convince anyone that Tony Sampson raped me? Mr. Sampson is going around telling everyone that we were in love. That it was consensual sex. I will admit I thought Tony was cute, but I never asked for this."

"No one has the right to touch another person without their consent. No means no! I don't care if you were a prostitute. If you didn't consent to sex, then it was rape!" Katie said, speaking a little louder than she wanted to.

"What if I didn't tell him no? Katie, I couldn't speak. He came into my room that night and started kissing me. Then he started taking off my nightgown. I was so shocked I just lay there. Plus, my mom had warned me to lock my door. I couldn't understand why she would say that. Now I know. I wanted to scream, Katie. I froze. I couldn't move. I couldn't believe this was happening to me! When he was done, he got up, looked back at me, and said, 'Nice.' I wanted to puke. I stayed in bed, crying, all night until my mom came into my bedroom. She asked me if I had taken a shower. I told her no, so she made me grab a coat, and we headed to the hospital. She said if I didn't shower, we could get DNA from the rape kit they do on you. After they were finished, my mom called the police. She asked them to meet us at the hospital. Katie, I'm no longer a virgin. I will never be able to give my husband that part of me. I hate Tony Sampson. I wish I would have locked my door. I wish Tony Sampson hadn't stayed overnight that night!"

Just then, Papa's watch started spinning out of control. The hourglass flipped, and Katie was outside the corner store. Monya was pumping gas in her mother's car. She ran over to Katie to thank her for giving her a second chance.

"Tonight's the night, Katie. I'm ahead of the game."

"You know you won't remember this after tonight, so just listen to your mom, okay?"

She nodded and happily walked back to her mom's car. "Bye, Katie!"

Katie waved and got into her car. By the time she got home, Nana's car was in the driveway. *Finally, I may be able to talk to her.* As she walked in the front door, Teddy was there to greet her. He started barking and jumping up and down. "You want a treat, boy?"

Katie went to the closet to hang up her coat. She grabbed Teddy a treat, and Nana came from the kitchen with flour all over her.

"Did you get into a fight with the flour bag? Looks like he won," Katie said, giggling.

"I'm trying to make some bread, Smarty-pants."

Katie followed Nana into the kitchen, and sure enough, there was flour all over. There was a cloud of flour covering the back door. Nana asked Katie to follow her. It was dark outside, which was weird, because it had been light when she'd driven into the driveway. There was a light near the swing. Katie walked over, and Nana told her to sit down and said there was someone there to see her. She was gone, and there was a bright light coming toward Katie.

"Oh my gosh! Papa! Where? How?" Katie stood up, but he told her to sit down. She gave him a big hug. "I've missed you so much, Papa. There is so much I need to know. I don't even know where to start. Where did Nana go?"

"Don't worry; she will be back to get you when it's time."

"Papa, I know you left me the watch, but I'm not sure I'm the right person to carry on the responsibilities. I'm scared, Papa."

"Don't doubt yourself, Katie. You are strong enough. If I didn't think you were, you wouldn't be wearing the watch."

"Why does it pick some people to help and leave others to their stories to work themselves out?"

"As you may have noticed, Sweetie, there are some forces of nature you can't mess with. Especially death. We have no control over that part of life. When a person's journey is completed here, that's when he or she is taken home."

"What about the people with different diseases? There are some people I can help and others I can't."

"Remember, Katie, you are not in charge. You were given a gift that helps people, but in the end, it really is out of our hands. That was my problem. I could help people, but I couldn't help myself. If you allow yourself to get caught up with the whys, you'll be no good for anyone. Just be grateful for the ones you can help, and focus on those people. Last thing, Katie, there are a bunch of notebooks that I left in the basement to help you out. What you need to do for the next watch bearer is to start writing for him or her. You'll know who to pass the watch on to next when the time comes. I don't have much longer. Take care of your nana for me."

"Will I see you again?"

"I don't know, Sweetheart. You might, but I don't make the rules. I love you."

It was dark. All Katie heard was beeping all around her. A big gust of wind hit her face, and she was back at the BSU.

"There you are, Katie! I asked you to speak to the new kid—Brody," Cathy said. "All that kid does is ring that damn nurses' bell. Could you please have a talk with him?"

"Sure, Cathy."

Katie walked into the TV room and didn't see anyone. Then she saw the nurses' call light over Brody's door. She went to his room and shut off the call button.

"Hi. My name is Katie. What's yours?" she asked, even though she knew his name.

"Brody."

"Well, Brody, I'm here to help you. What seems to be the problem? You keep ringing the nurses' bell."

"I want to go home! I don't want to be here anymore. I'm not crazy."

"Can I ask you why you were sent here?"

"Why should I trust you? Who are you?"

She told him who she was and said she was there to help him.

"Why should I trust you?" he asked again.

"Well, you're going to have to trust someone. Or they will keep you here until you do. You need to talk to somebody, Brody. Do me a favor." She reached into her bag and pulled out an envelope, a piece of paper, and a pen. "Can you write down something on this piece of paper that you have never told anyone before? Then, when you're done, put it inside the envelope, and give it back to me."

He gave her a weird look but started writing on the paper. He then put it in the envelope and sealed it. He handed her the envelope. She ripped up the envelope and said, "See? You do trust me."

"Why did you rip up the envelope?"

"I wanted to know if you trusted me enough to talk to me. So, I just got my answer."

"Oh, it was a test."

"Yes, it was. You have to trust the person you are talking to, or else they can't help you solve any of your problems."

Both of his hands were bandaged.

"Do you want to tell me about the bandages on your hands? Is that what brought you in here?"

He looked down at his hands and said, "Kind of. You're not a nurse or a doctor. How are you going to help me?"

"No, I am a counselor. I listen to what you have to say, and then I report back to my boss, who in turn gives information to other counselors who may have had a client like you. We share information to help each other."

"You mean there are other people like me?"

"Well, I'm not sure. I don't know what you're dealing with yet."

"Okay, I think I'm ready to talk to you, Katie. Where to begin?"

"Why don't you start with what brought you here?"

Brody looked at the floor and started talking. "I burned my hands on the stove in my mom's kitchen."

"Brody, why would you do that?"

"I had to! Don't you see? Every time I think about Pastor Joe, I have to burn myself. That's what my mother did the first time I told her about Pastor Joe."

"Why would your mother burn your hands? What did you say to her?"

"I told her Pastor Joe touched me. She called me a liar and said I was telling stories that shouldn't be told. Then she took me over to the stove and burned both of my hands. I was ten years old when it first happened. Pastor Joe asked me to help him clean the church after prayer service. He grabbed me between the legs when I went to hang up my coat. I wanted to run, but I froze. I was in shock that he would touch me there. I found my voice and asked him not to touch me there, but he said all the boys my age like it. If I didn't want to be one of his boys, I could leave. I really thought I was missing out on what the other boys my age was doing with Pastor Joe, but I was scared. I ran home to tell my mom. Unfortunately, she was at work. Ever since my dad left us, she's had to work more hours at the diner. My brother, Jimmy, was home. I told him what happened. He told me not to tell Mom. She would just get mad at me. I asked him if he was ever touched by Pastor Joe. He showed me his hands and said yes. I thought Pastor Joe did something to my brother's hands. My mother was always saying Jimmy was just like his father—nothing but a troublemaker.

"I soon found out that it wasn't Pastor Joe who burnt Jimmy's hands. It was my mom who burnt his hands. She said that Pastor Joe was helping us pay for our rent. That I shouldn't spread such rumors about such a godly man who was just trying to help. The next three years were like a game we played. I would stay after church services, and Pastor Joe and I would play touching games with each other. It wasn't until I turned thirteen that he no longer wanted anything to do with me. I think I love him, Katie. But he doesn't want anything to do with me. He even told my mom that if she brought me back to church, he would quit helping her make her rent payments."

"When my mother asked why, Pastor Joe said I was crazy. Anyone who is crazy must have demons inside them, and he didn't want any demons in his church. Now I'm all alone. Jimmy ran away, and I don't have anyone. My mother looks at me in a disgusted way, I'm not allowed back in church, and I don't have any friends. The day I got put in here, Tom, our neighbor, came over to our trailer and found me burning my hands on the stove. I guess I was screaming loud for Tom to hear me. He dialed 911, and I ended up in the BSU. I wish I'd never helped Pastor Joe clean up after services."

Katie thought Papa's watch was going to take them back, but it didn't move. "Brody, I need to speak with other people about your situation. Pastor Joe can't keep doing this to young boys. I'm sure you and your brother are not the only ones. What he did was wrong!" she said with a lot of anger. "You may feel like you're in love with him, but that's not love, Brody. That's an older man taking advantage of a young man. It's called pedophilia."

"I know now what it is, Katie, but my mom won't get any more help paying the rent if I tell on him."

"Brody, if you don't say something, he will continue to do this to other young boys. I will get people to help you and your mom. I would like to talk with Dr. Faulk, with your permission."

Brody nodded.

"I will be right back." Katie walked out of his room and into the TV lounge to catch her breath. She was so angry that she needed to calm down a bit before she went in to see the doctor. "Deep breaths, Katie," she said to herself. She ran into Raymie at the nurses' station. "Hey, Raymie, is Dr. Faulk here?"

"No, he left for the day and won't be back in until seven o'clock tomorrow morning. What can I help you with?"

"I really need to talk to Dr. Faulk. He's the only one Brody gave me permission to talk to."

"Dr. Brannish is covering for Dr. Faulk. Do you want me to try to get ahold of him?"

"No, I will let Brody know he's back in the morning."

Katie went back to the children's ward and looked into Brody's room. She couldn't find him. He wasn't in the TV lounge either. She went back to the nurses' station and asked if anyone had seen Brody. Raymie insisted he had to be in his room and said she was going to look in there. The next thing Katie heard was "Code blue in children's ward! Code blue in children's ward!"

Katie ran back to the ward.

Raymie came running up to her. "My God, Katie, what happened? What did you say to him?"

"I told him I was going to go get some help. That I would be right back."

"Well, no one can help him now, Katie. Brody is dead."

"But how? They don't have anything in their rooms."

"Is this yours, Katie?" She showed Katie a scarf.

"Oh my God!"

Just then, everything went black. Suddenly, Papa was in front of her.

"Papa, I can't do this anymore. It's just too hard, and it hurts too much."

"You don't have to, Katie; it's time for you to come with me."

"Are we going back to Nana's?"

"No, you are coming with me. You've been through enough."

"Wait—are you telling me what I think you're telling me?"

"Yes, Katie, it's time for you to pass the watch."

"No, Papa, I can do this. Please don't take me. I need to be with Nana. I need to take care of her."

"Katie, you don't need to take care of anyone. You've done enough."

They started to walk through the fog, when Katie heard Nana. She was crying.

"Katie, please, honey, come back to us."

Katie felt herself falling. She was in a hospital room. She remembered what had taken place. Brody was gone. He was dead. *I'm responsible for his death. It was my scarf.* Just then, the door opened. Nana and Jamie walked into the room.

"Katie, you're awake. We've been here for over an hour, and no one has come into your room to let us know what's going on. We went to the cafeteria to grab some coffee," Nana said.

"Katie, I'm so sorry." Jamie looked at her with tears in her eyes.

"Nana, I can't do anything right. Did you hear about the young man from upstairs?" Katie said with tears in her eyes.

"Yes, we heard. Katie, it's not your fault. He would have found something else to use. The young man wanted to end his journey. It wasn't up to you to stop it."

"You sound like Papa."

Jamie looked at Katie as if she had two heads. She knew Katie's grandfather had passed away and wondered why she would bring up his name as if she'd talked to him yesterday.

"Jamie, we have a lot of catching up to do as soon as I get out of here. Nana, could you call my boss? I must speak to her as soon as possible. Tonight, if possible."

Nana left the room to use the phone at the nurses' station.

"Katie, I thought we'd lost you for good this time. Dr. Brannish said you hit your head hard. I remember what he told you before you got released from the hospital the last time you were here." Jamie reached over the side of the bed to give Katie a hug. She hit her elbow on the rail. "Geez, O'Reilly, every time I try to hug you, I get hurt."

They giggled together, and she hugged Katie harder. The door flew open. It was Nana.

"Katie, your boss, Holly, can't make it in tonight; her daughter is sick. I think you'd better get some rest. We will be back tomorrow. Try to get some sleep, Sweetie. C'mon, Jamie!"

Katie gave Nana a kiss goodbye and hugged Jamie again. The door flew open, and Dr. Brannish walked in. "Mrs. O'Reilly, how are you this evening?"

"Better than Katie. How are you?"

"I'm doing well. Thank you for asking."

Jamie looked at Dr. Brannish with googly eyes. "Hello, Doctor."

"Evening, Jamie. Well, Katie, you seem to be in good hands tonight. I'm just checking in on you before I do my rounds."

"Thank you, Doctor. I appreciate it. It's been quite a rough day."

"Yes, I heard. I'm so sorry, Katie. It will get better. It's never easy when we lose a patient. But understanding that it wasn't your fault is the first step of healing. If there is anything, I can do to help you, let me know."

"Thank you, Doctor. I will. Nana and Jamie were just leaving."

Nana grabbed Jamie by the shirttail. "Yes, we were about to go. We will see you in the morning, Sweetie."

Jamie looked back at Katie and gave her a wink. "Bye, O'Reilly. Try to get some sleep. I will see you tomorrow."

"I'm leaving also, but if you need anything, Katie, let me know," Dr. Brannish said.

They all walked out together and left her by herself. Katie started crying, wondering if there was anything she could have done differently. *I know Papa's watch can't reverse death, but I wish I hadn't left my scarf. I know he could have used a pillowcase or something else. Why did it have to be my scarf?* Thankfully, sleep came quickly.

The next thing Katie knew, the light was shining into her room. She sat up and looked around. She almost had forgotten that she was in the hospital. She felt sad and angry. She needed to get justice for Brody. *I need to speak with my boss. She must help me get Pastor Joe. Brody was tortured by this monster.* The nurse's aide walked in with breakfast. Katie hadn't realized how hungry she was.

As she finished her breakfast, Holly came into the room. "Good morning, Katie. Did your nana explain to you why I couldn't come in last night?"

"Yes, she told me your daughter was sick. Is she feeling better today?"

"Yes, thank you. What can I help you with, Katie?"

"Well, did you hear about Brody?"

"Yes, and I'm so sorry. It's the worst part of this job, losing a patient by self-infliction or by a victim's significant other."

"I want to tell you why he took his life. Holly, you know Pastor Joe, right?" Katie knew he was the head of the church Holly attended.

"Yes, I do. Why do you ask?"

"Brody told me that Pastor Joe had been sexually assaulting him for the last three years. When he turned thirteen, he was told he wasn't needed anymore.

"That's a serious accusation, Katie."

"You know the man. Have you ever heard of anything like this before?"

"Well, there were rumors about Tobin's brother, Jimmy. Jimmy told Patrick my son, that Pastor Joe tried touching him.

We all thought Jimmy was mad at Pastor Joe for having to attend church. Everyone knew Jimmy didn't like going to church. He didn't like Pastor Joe. Jimmy is a big kid. A lot stronger than most kids his age. We just thought he wanted to be a tough guy by not coming to church."

"I'm pretty sure that's why Jimmy ran away. Brody told me Pastor Joe tried the same thing when he was younger. I guess maybe the kid, being as big as he was, thought that Pastor Joe wasn't going to mess with him. Have you heard any rumors about where Jimmy could have gone?"

"Some say he went to Florida to look for his biological father. His mother's new boyfriend is a real loser. He's a drunk and a troublemaker."

"I really don't understand people like their mother. Brody told her about Pastor Joe. Apparently, he has been helping her pay her rent, so she did nothing to stop the problem. Do you think she will talk now? What if he has another young boy he's doing this to? It sounds like he's targeting kids who come from poor families, and that's how he's getting away with this. We need to do something, Holly."

"Well, short of finding Jimmy, we have nothing. No one has come forward with any accusations."

"I feel as if I need to get justice for Brody, Holly. His death was caused by Pastor Joe's abuse. If Jimmy shows up for his brother's funeral, I am going to ask him to talk to the police. Do I have your permission?"

"Do what you need to do, Katie. If Pastor Joe is a pedophile, we need to take him down."

"Thanks, Holly. I'm going to go home today to get some work finished for school. Graduation is a month away. I've completed all my studies, but I have paperwork I need to complete for college. I will talk to you tomorrow."

Katie went to the breakroom to get her coat. Just then, she saw Tim, the maintenance man. "Hey, Tim. Thanks for cleaning my locker the other day."

"Well, Katie, I've been meaning to speak to you about that. Someone must have gotten to your locker before I did. When I went in, there was no mouse in your locker. I'm not sure who would have taken care of it, but you'll have to thank someone else."

She thanked him again, grabbed her coat, and headed for the elevator. She caught a glimpse of a young girl sitting in a wheelchair with her head down. The girl looked up, and Katie thought she saw red eyes. She looked down at her shoes, and Papa's watch started burning her arm. *This can't be good*, she thought to herself. She wanted to know more about the girl, but Katie was too mentally exhausted to talk to anyone else that day. She slipped inside the elevator, and down she went.

Katie ran into Tammy, but she was on the phone, so Katie waved goodbye and headed for her car. She drove slowly home, thinking about everything that had taken place in the last few days. *Why would I be seeing things that aren't there? What does this all mean?*

As she drove into the driveway, Katie saw Nana's car. She was happy, as she didn't want to be alone. She ran into the house, and Teddy was there to greet her. His tail swung back and forth fast, and he gave her a lick on her face. He was clearly happy she was home. Nana was sitting at the table, reading her Bible. She looked up when Katie entered the room.

"Katie, I didn't know you were coming home this morning. I could have come to the hospital to pick you up."

"I'm fine, Nana. Thank you, though."

"Let me make you a nice cup of tea and honey."

Nana went to the kitchen while Katie hung up her coat and put on her slippers. Nana brought the tea to her.

"Katie, I think it's time you start digging into your papa's notebooks he left you. You've been through a lot. You might find something in there that could help you. Or if you decide it is too much for you, you may just close them and find someone else to be the watch keeper. I wouldn't blame you. But I want you to know I believe in you."

"Thank you, Nana. That means a lot to me. I think I'm going to go lie down for a while. I will read them a little later."

"I will bring them up to you, sweetheart. Go lie down for now."

Katie headed upstairs with Teddy following right behind. She lay down on her bed, and as much as she wanted to read Papa's notebooks, sleep took over.

It was late in the afternoon when she woke up. As promised, Papa's notebooks were piled in the corner of her room. She reached for the top one and opened it: "The Beginning" by Kevin O'Reilly. It was weird to look at her grandfather's handwriting. But she started reading.

CHAPTER 12

The Notebook

Day One: Today I received the watch from Uncle Ken. It didn't come with any specific instructions, but there were some notebooks that came with it. It seems that the watch has been passed down through generations of O'Reillys. Each new keeper receives the watch and the writings of *only the immediately previous keeper*. So, along with the responsibility of the watch, the new keeper must take detailed notes for the next keeper. Uncle Ken said that I would learn from the watch itself, and I would need to read the notebooks to help me understand its incredible power.

Lately I have been experiencing emotions that I have never felt before, especially around certain people. It's then that the watch burns my arm. Not like it would if I scorched myself on a stove or fire, but an intense warming happens that I just can't ignore. I'm not sure what it means, but I know something is not right. Something bad is about to happen.

My first encounter with the watch was one day while I was visiting my grandfather. I became good friends with Maggie, a girl who lived down the road from my grandfather's farm. Maggie and her father lived in a what could only be called a shack. Maggie's mother died when Maggie was only eight years old. Her father started drinking a lot after his wife passed. Maggie was given the choice to stay with her father or go to live with her aunt. She chose to stay with her dad. She thought he needed someone to take care of him. As the summer days passed, Maggie would visit me, and she would have bruises on her arms and legs. I would ask her about them, but she always had an excuse. I always thought something was going on in her house, but she would never tell me.

One day Maggie ran up the dusty road toward me. I was outside, feeding the horses hay, and she collapsed in my arms. Her clothes were ripped, and she told me her father had attacked her. I was so angry. I wanted to find her father and hurt him bad. She said something then that made the watch spin out of control, and the hourglass turned upside down. Time had shifted, and the awful events of the day had never happened. Maggie could now go to her aunt before they did. She came back to Grandpa's house and thanked me. We said our good-byes. The next day, she didn't remember me.

As Katie read through Papa's stories, she got angry. *How come I wasn't warned or told anything about the watch when I took it over? I just got, "You're strong enough, Katie; you'll know what to do." I had to figure out all this craziness for myself.* Katie wondered how many people were told about the watch before they got it. She closed the notebook and headed downstairs. She was hungry and could smell Nana's cooking. She asked Nana, "Why were some people warned about the watch, and other people were just given the watch? I didn't have that advantage."

Nana looked at her while she spewed question after question. "Katie, you need to slow down! I can't answer these questions because I don't know. The only thing I can tell you is that only the strongest people are handed the watch. If your grandfather didn't think you could handle it, he would have passed it on to someone else. I know your papa went through hell while he wore that watch. Sometimes he was happy to take on the responsibilities of the watch, especially in the beginning. It really was a source of healing for so many, and Papa got such satisfaction in helping." She spoke with more emotion than Katie was ready for. "Katie, read the notebooks. Also, remember, you need to write in notebooks for the next person who will take the watch over."

"Thank you, Nana. I appreciate all your help."

"Why don't you sit down, Katie? Dinner is almost ready."

Katie got up and helped Nana set the table. Nana went to warm her coffee in the microwave. Suddenly, a foul smell hit Katie's and Nana's noses.

"Oh my gosh, what is that smell?" Nana said.

Katie remembered she had left hamburger in the microwave. "Nana, I put that in to defrost the other night. I'm sorry I left it there." She pulled the burger out, and maggots were all over it. The turntable had hundreds of nasty bugs around it. She threw the burger in the garbage and ran the turntable under water. The maggots fell into the garbage disposal. She put the garbage bag outside, and Nana sprayed the garbage can with Lysol. "I'm so sorry for wasting all that hamburger, Nana. I totally forgot about it when I got called into work."

"Don't worry about it, sweetie. No use crying over spoiled meat." They both giggled and sat down to eat.

After dinner, Katie started cleaning and told Nana to go sit down. She loaded the dishwasher and put away the leftovers. She then went to sit with Nana, but she heard the shower running. *She must be tired of all the questions I've thrown at her.* That was Katie's cue that Nana was going to bed. Katie was tired too, so she climbed the stairs with Teddy on her heels behind her. She wanted to read more of the notebooks, but she was too tired.

Morning came with the sun shining in her eyes. She slept in later than usual. She thought she would reach out to Holly to ask her about work. *I should get back. Sitting around is not doing anything for me except making me think too much about the what-ifs.* She picked up the phone and called her. After she got off the phone, she decided to go into work. She felt refreshed, and she needed to put her mind on something else. She showered and went into the kitchen to grab coffee and a bagel. Nana had left for work. Katie climbed into her car, and off she went.

When she got to the BSU, she felt a sense of regret. *I probably jumped the gun by coming to work so soon.* All the emotions of losing Brody and the rest of the kids she'd helped came into her head. She was a little overwhelmed by them all. *I wonder how they are doing. I wonder where Jimmy is and if he is going to show up at the funeral.*

Suddenly, she looked in her rearview mirror and saw him—the guy she had run into that night at the restaurant. She decided to follow the SUV.

She didn't want him to see her, so she stayed a few cars back. She followed the vehicle until it came to a stop outside the house next to the Sampson's house. She drove by but not before watching him get out of his car. She now knew where the man of her dreams lived. *I didn't make him up. Sooner or later, I will meet him.* She drove slowly back to the BSU.

CHAPTER 13

The Visit

H.G. was sitting in his study, at his desk, when he called Tony into his office. "So, Son, this practice game this weekend is going to be huge. I heard there will be scouts all over the bleachers. You need to make sure you're giving your top performance, mister."

"Yes, sir." Tony rolled his eyes. He wanted to go into the marines, but his father had other plans for him. He also liked Monya Sanchez, his buddy Mike's little sister, but that was never going to happen. Mr. Sanchez worked for his father. God forbid any of his children should date one of those lowlifes, as H.G. referred to them. They were the very people who'd made his father a wealthy man. He didn't appreciate them as he should have. Maybe that night after the game, he could talk to Monya.

"All right, buddy, go fill up on carbs. You're going to need all you can get. Keep your strength up. And go find your sister. I need to speak to her."

Tony left his study to go find Edith. She was in her room, listening to music with her headphones on.

Tony nudged her foot. "Hey, squirt, Dad wants to talk to you."

Edith got up, rolling her eyes. "What now? Does he want to keep Mom away for longer?"

"I don't know what he wants to talk to you about. He just asked me to find you."

Edith got up from her bed and walked down to her father's study. "Hi, Daddy. Tony said you wanted to see me?"

"Yeah, Edie, whatever happened to that Haul girl who goes to your school?"

"You mean Penny?" She gave her father a weird look, wondering why on earth he would be asking about the town's hippie.

"Is that her name? Well, I need to talk to her grandmother about some property she owns. Not that it's any of your business, Edith."

"Dad, you can't go around asking me about a weirdo who goes to my school without my wondering why."

"Edith, not that it's any of your business, but rumor has it Penny's grandmother has deeded all her land to her granddaughter. If I am to get any of the property, I need to speak to Penny. That's her name, right?"

"Yes, Dad. That is her name. You won't be able to talk to her until later. She goes to the cemetery every day after school to visit her parents. Kids at school tease her about it. They say crap like, 'Your friends are real deadbeats.' Crap like that. But I wouldn't mess with that family, Dad. Rumors have it that her grandmother is evil. She dabbles in stuff from the dark side."

"What on earth are you talking about?"

"They say she's a witch! Strange things happen to kids who make fun of Penny. But if you're interested, I saw her go to the cemetery after school. If you hurry, you'll be able to catch her."

"Very funny, young lady. I need to speak to both Haul women. I don't think they'll both be there."

She giggled and left the room. Edith was the apple of his eye. Tony was next; he was up for an athletic scholarship to Penn State. Tony was following in his footsteps. Then he had Peter and Tommy. Peter was nothing but a troublemaker. Hurting that Knapp kid at school was going to cost his family dearly. Jack wasn't going to let it go, especially since his wife had died. Tommy, his youngest, was a scrawny kid who had little ambition. He kind of reminded H.G. of himself when he was younger.

H.G. got up and went to the dining room to have dinner with his family. Ever since Kimberly had gone into rehab, Cindy had taken over a lot more responsibilities around the house.

"Good evening, Mr. Sampson." Cindy greeted him with her eyes toward the floor.

"Oh, for heaven's sake, Cindy, how many times must I tell you to call me H.G.?"

"Yes, Mr.—I mean H.G. Dinner is ready."

"Cindy, can you stay a little later tonight? I need to go out, and I don't want the kids to leave the house."

"Yes, sir. I mean H.G."

"Thank you, Cindy."

Tommy, Edith, Tony, and Peter were all sitting at the

table for dinner. Their father was strict when it came to dinner. Everyone needed to be at the table. Tony started talking to his dad when he came in the door.

"Hey, Dad, I just got off the phone with Coach Morse. He confirmed the rumors about the scouts being at the game this weekend."

"That's great news. You'll show them all up." He then turned to Peter. "As soon as the dust settles, you are going to live with your uncle and aunt in California."

Peter knew better than to argue with his father.

Edith piped into the conversation. "When is Mom coming home?" She knew better than to bring up her mother, but she missed her.

H.G. looked at her with daggers. "She will come home when she decides to quit drinking for good!" he said grumpily.

Edith went back to eating. Tommy didn't say anything. He was afraid of his mother.

"I want all of you to stay in tonight. I'm going out for a while, and I don't want to hear that any of you have left this house. You'd better have all your homework done. Cindy will be here, and she will let me know if any of you step one foot out of here."

"Yes, Father," they all said in unison.

H.G. got up from the table, grabbed his briefcase and his coat from his study, and walked out the door. He was going to go see the woman Edith had called a witch. H.G. climbed into his Hummer. The Hauls lived on a dirt road, and he didn't want to get his BMW dirty. He drove down Route 6 to Route 220. The old woman lived in a run-down house, but the property the house was sitting on was a gold mine. The property had natural gas that the gas companies could tap into. The road leading to the house was bumpy and full of potholes, but H.G. wanted something, and he wasn't going to let any obstacles get in his way.

When he arrived, two pit bulls were outside the house, barking. It was a large Victorian house with stained-glass windows. It needed a good paint job. It looked kind of spooky. He didn't dare get out of his car, even if the dogs were chained up. He seemed to have to sit there for quite a while before an older woman came out the front door to yell at her dogs. They immediately calmed down. She looked at the vehicle and knew who was inside. He stepped out of his car and looked right at her.

"Gracie, you know why I'm here."

"I do, H.G., and you're not getting it!"

"If you don't give it to me now, eventually, I will get it. You might have an accident, or your house might burn down with you in it."

She grabbed ahold of her locket. "Are you threatening me? This has already helped you once. If you aren't careful, I will take it back." She had used the locket to get him off on a DUI and vehicular homicide charge. The bastard had killed a young girl, and she knew he was guilty, but she'd wanted money from him.

He thought about her property and how much money he could make off it, but more than that, he wanted the locket.

"H.G., you need to leave right now. If you don't, I'm sure Officer Knapp would love to haul you to jail."

He knew he shouldn't mess with Gracie. He certainly didn't want the cops involved in his affairs. He couldn't afford that.

"I'll be watching you, Gracie. Oh, and you'd better watch your granddaughter. Penny, right?"

"You wouldn't dare!"

"I'm leaving for now." H.G. got in his car and took off.

Penny came to the door after H.G. left. "Grandma, what was that all about?"

"Nothing. Go back inside."

Penny was cleaning the kitchen when Gracie walked in. "Grandma, I heard you and Mr. Sampson talking. Why would he threaten us over a piece of jewelry?"

"Penny, this locket is not just a piece of jewelry. Unfortunately, this locket has helped a lot of bad people out of a lot of bad situations. It's also helped a lot of good people get into bad situations. But never mind that now. You have nothing to worry about. If I have this locket, we will be okay."

"You are not making sense, Grandma."

"Well, a few years back, I helped H.G. get out of a DUI charge."

"How did you do it?"

"I opened the locket and commanded his blood-alcohol files into the locket. The officer on duty was blamed for losing his files. But as it stands, they're here in this locket. I felt horrible about the young girl who died. When I met the mother, I decided I would no longer use the locket to get a hardened criminal off. I have used it to make some people sick every now and again but not in the way I did back then. If I hadn't helped H.G., he would still be in jail today. Apparently, the locket has a sister, so to speak. It is used to do good. It's not a locket but a watch."

H.G. was furious. He needed to figure out a way to get rid

of Gracie Haul. By rights, that locket belonged to him and his family. If she wasn't going to use the locket, he would figure out a way to get it and use it. As he drove home, he thought about the night he'd left the bar and killed that young girl.

H.G. knew he should have taken a taxi, but he had picked up a prostitute and wanted to have a little fun with her. The road was deserted, and Crystal's hands felt so good that H.G. closed his eyes for just a second. The little girl came out of nowhere, and before anyone knew what had happened, she was run over. The prostitute ran away from the scene of the accident, and H.G. was hauled away by Officer Scott. Their first stop was the hospital. They took his blood to determine an alcohol level. It was way over the legal limit, and H.G. was booked that night. Peter Sampson wasn't happy with his son and that he would disgrace his name in that manner. He contacted an attorney from New York City. The little girl died in the hospital two days later. H.G. was facing vehicular homicide.

He had heard about the locket from his father. His father said that it was theirs. "But your idiot grandmother gave it to Gracie's mother as a gift when she was pregnant with Gracie." H.G. knew the locket was powerful, so he went to see Gracie. She told H.G. she needed $100,000 to get him out of trouble. H.G. was curious how she was going to help him get out of this one.

She told him to give her $50,000 now. "And after a couple days, you'll get your answer, and you can pay me the rest."

He did as he was instructed. He paid her the money, and by the time he got home, his lawyer had contacted him to say they'd lost his blood-alcohol files. They couldn't charge him for the homicide. He immediately went to Gracie and paid her the other half that was due.

Coming back to the present, H.G. pulled into the driveway and saw that Cindy was still there. He told her to have a good night and walked into his study. He called the older kids in to talk to him.

"Edith, you know Penny Haul. What grade is she in?"

"She's a junior this year; she is in classes with Tony."

"Who are you talking about?" Tony asked.

"Penny Haul, the one with the dreadlocks."

"Dad, why do you want to know about that crazy chick?"

"I want you kids to get to know her."

"What?" Tony and Edith said at the same time.

"Daddy, I think Tony should," Edith said. "She's in his class. I don't see her other than walking through the halls." She hoped her father wouldn't embarrass her like that.

"No way, Dad. Are you trying to embarrass the shit out of me?"

"I'll do it!" Peter piped up. "She's a year behind me; she will talk to me."

"Okay. It's settled. Don't screw this up, Peter. I'm asking you to do this one thing for me. Don't let me down, Son."

It was the first time H.G. had called Peter Son. Peter wasn't going to let his father down.

CHAPTER 14

Penny

Peter drove to school and waited in the parking lot for Penny. Just as the first bell rang, Penny walked close by. Peter bent down and pretended to tie his shoe. He looked up just as Penny walked by him.

"Hi!"

Penny looked behind her to see who Peter Sampson was talking to. When she didn't see anyone, she said, "Are you talking to me?"

"Well, do you see anyone else behind you?"

"No, but why would you say hi to me?"

"You look like you need a friendly person in your life."

"You think so, huh?"

"Can I walk you to your class?"

"Sure."

They walked into school side by side. Peter knew he was

going to catch some crap for being with Penny "Dreadlock" Haul, but he wasn't about to let his dad down.

"Hey, do you have classes with my brother Tony?"

"Yes, he is in my world history class and my English class." She doubted he even knew she existed.

"What other classes are you taking?"

"Precalculus, Anatomy 101, and Life Skills."

"What do you want to do after high school?"

"I'm not sure. I know if I'm going to college, I should start applying, but I'm just not sure what I want with my life. I've been taking classes that are required for entering college. I just don't know what I want to do or where I want to go. What are you doing next year?"

"If my father has his way, I will be living in California with my aunt and uncle. I'd like to join the military, but that's out of the question for my father. He says uneducated people join the military."

"That's a horrible way to think. I know quite a few very intelligent people who went into the military. They were able to take advantage of incredible educational opportunities through the service."

"Don't get me wrong. I don't think that way. I'm a high honors student, and I still want to join the military. A lot of people have no idea what it's like to live in the Sampson house. My dad is tougher on his boys than people think. Just because I'm a Sampson doesn't mean I get away with anything." Peter couldn't understand why he was telling Penny all this, but it was easy to talk to her.

"Here is my stop. I need to get inside before the next bell rings," she said.

"Okay, maybe we can talk after school. I like talking to you, Penny."

She liked how her name rolled off his tongue: Pen-knee. She thought it was cute. Penny sat through morning classes thinking about Peter. She couldn't understand why a senior boy would be talking to her, especially a Sampson.

The day seemed as if it would never end. Finally, the last bell rang, and she almost ran to her locker. He was standing behind her locker when she shut it.

"You scared me!" she said.

"Do you need a ride home?"

"No, I need to go somewhere. Thank you, though."

He looked disappointed. "Can I take you where you need to go?"

"No, I'm just walking over to the cemetery to visit my parents."

"Oh, I'm sorry about that."

"It's no biggie. I go every day to see them. I just don't want to miss being with them."

"I get it. Would you want some company?"

"Not today. Maybe another day."

"Okay. You want to meet me in the morning? The parking lots?"

"Yeah, okay. See you in the morning."

"Bye, Penny."

"Bye, Peter."

She walked down the hill and through town to get to the cemetery. She was in a good mood for a change. She was excited to tell her mom about Peter. She wasn't going to tell her grandmother, especially after last's night episode with H.G. She sat down near her parents' gravestone.

"Hi, Mom and Dad. Mom, I talked to a boy today. He's cute and smart. He seems sweet and kind too. I'm not sure when I will bring him here to meet you and Dad. We will have to see where this is going. I wish you were here, Mom. I really need your help. I'd like to clean up a bit, and I don't need Grandma asking me questions. I wish you were here. I think I'm going to go get some new clothes and get my hair fixed. With some of the money you and Dad left me, I could clean up pretty good. Yep. That's what I'm going to do. Thanks for listening. I'll see you two tomorrow."

She ran back home and grabbed money out of her safe. *A few hundred should do it.* Her grandmother wasn't home. She was happy about that. She didn't want to explain anything right now. She called a cab and went off to the mall. She arrived at the mall and wasn't sure where she was going to go. She had seen signs for salons all over but wasn't sure which one she should go into. She would ask which one knew how to take dreadlocks out of hair. She walked into the first one she saw. The lady behind the registration desk asked her what she wanted done.

"Can you get rid of these dreadlocks without shaving my head?"

"Yes, but let me ask if my assistant will stay to help. It's going to take a while." She went into the back and then came back out. "She said she would stay, but it's going to cost quite a bit."

"I'm not worried about the money; I have enough if you can do it."

"Yes, we can. Come on back."

They started by washing her hair and then conditioning it. Then they combed each dreadlock one at a time from the bottom of her hair up. Penny helped with the front dreads. It took about two hours before they finished her hair.

"Do you want me to style your hair?"

"Yes, please!"

Penny was so excited she could hardly speak. After another half hour, she was ready to walk out of the salon.

"You're a really pretty girl. Of course, now that we can see your face."

Penny started crying. She hadn't felt pretty in a long time. "Thank you, guys. I really appreciate the fact that you were able to keep the length."

"No problem. You have gorgeous hair!"

Penny paid them and gave them each a twenty-dollar tip. She promised to see them again soon. She wanted to buy new clothes but didn't want to deviate from her style too much. Most of her clothes came from Hot Bottoms, but she wanted to go a little less goth and more country. She went into American Pelicans. She always liked the look of their ads. Georgia, a girl she went to school with, was working near the cash register. Georgia approached Penny and asked her if she could help her find anything. Penny knew Georgia didn't recognize her.

"I'm looking for a couple outfits. Probably jeans and a flannel."

"We just got some new items in; let me show you." She picked out a red-and-black plaid shirt and a gray-and-navy plaid shirt. "What style of jeans are you looking for? We have boot cut, curvy, skinny, and flare."

"I'd like to try on a boot-cut style."

Georgia asked her what size she wore and grabbed them

off the wall. Penny took the clothes into the dressing room and liked what she saw.

"I'll take both of them," she said, coming up to the register. She also grabbed a couple Henleys off the racks. Georgia rang up her purchases, and off she went.

The next stop was the nail salon. Her nails were painted black and chipping. *Why not?* She walked over to the nail salon, signed in, and waited for her name to be called. Edith and her friends were getting their nails done, and they looked at Penny as if they had seen her before but were not quite sure where. Her name was called, and she sat down with her back toward them. She explained to the lady that she wanted her nails done like the poster on the wall. It was a French manicure.

"You want white tips and gel?"

"Sure."

They finished her nails, and she was hungry. She started up the escalator to the food court. After looking at all the options, she settled on ordering a slice of pizza.

Suddenly, she spotted Peter, but she didn't want him to see her just yet. She grabbed her plate, threw away a partially eaten piece of pizza, and ran into the ladies' room. She stayed in the restroom for fifteen minutes and then thought, *Here goes nothing.* She walked out of the restroom and bumped right into Peter.

"Excuse me," she said.

"Penny?"

"Yes, Peter. It's me."

"Wow, you look different," he said, stuttering.

"Is that a good thing or a bad thing?"

"Oh, it's a good thing. I mean, you looked good before, but you really look different. Have you eaten?"

"Yes, I was just about ready to leave."

"Do you need a ride?"

"No, my grandmother is picking me up," she lied.

She wasn't ready for her grandmother's questions about her appearance. She would call a cab once she was out of Peter's sight.

"Okay. I'll see you in the parking lot tomorrow?"

"I'll be there. See you later."

She walked off and went down the escalator, looking back at Peter. As soon as she was out of his sight, she called for a taxi. She asked them to pick her up out behind the mall. On her way home, she thought about Peter and how he'd reacted to the new Penny. She liked it.

They pulled into her driveway, and she thought about what she was going to tell her grandmother. *Unfortunately, I can't get much past her.* She was going to see right through her. She paid the cab driver and told him to keep the change.

"Thank you, miss."

She walked up to the front porch. The light was on, but she hadn't spotted her grandmother. She walked into the hall and ran up the stairs with her packages.

"Penny, is that you, dear?"

"Yes, Grandma, I'm tired, and I'm going to bed."

"Did you eat?"

"I grabbed something while I was out. Thanks."

"All right, good night, sweetie. I'll see you in the morning."

"Goodnight, Grandma."

Penny woke up before her alarm went off. She searched in

her closet for her mother's makeup bag. She'd thought about having her grandmother throw it out when her mom passed. She was happy she hadn't. She just wanted some mascara and blush. She pulled the bag out and realized there was a lot more to make up than she'd ever thought. *All these brushes. All these colors.* She was going to have to watch some makeup tutorials. She kept her hair up, put on a hat, and went down for breakfast.

"Good morning, Grandma."

"Good morning, Pen—okay, what's going on here?"

"What do you mean?" Although Penny knew what her grandmother was talking about, she wasn't going to make it easy for her.

"Please take that hat off. I'm sure you'll want to show off your new hairdo."

Penny slowly took off her hat.

"Oh, thank God you finally got rid of those nasty dreadlocks. I'm not sure why the change suddenly, but when you're ready to talk to me, I'm here."

Penny was happy she didn't have to explain the change in her appearance or get the third degree. She drank her orange juice and ate her toast. She got up from the table, put her glass in the sink, and kissed her grandma goodbye. Penny was happy for the first time since her parents had passed away. She felt good. She walked faster than she had in a long time to school. When she got to the parking lot, she saw Peter. He was waiting near his car. She heard a group of boys whistling at her. Peter looked up and caught Penny's eye. He hadn't realized how beautiful she was. He'd thought she was yesterday when he talked to her, but she was stunning. Penny walked up to Peter and greeted him.

"Hi," he said, a little shy. He couldn't understand why he felt that way suddenly.

"How was your night?" she asked, feeling his awkwardness.

"It was good. Can I walk you to class?"

The first bell rang, and they walked in silence. The people who'd been pointing and laughing yesterday when they walked together were quiet and whispering among each other.

"Well, this is my stop," she said.

"Do you want to go for a soda or something after you visit your parents?"

"I really need to get home today. I kind of ditched my grandma last night without telling her where I was going. Maybe we could go tomorrow?"

"Okay, great. It's a deal."

"See you later."

"Sure, at least in the parking lot tomorrow."

The second bell rang, and they went their separate ways. She walked into American History, and Tony Sampson looked at her in shock. *I guess I should have told my father I would get to know her,* he thought. A bunch of guys, including Tony, surrounded Penny.

"You a new girl in town?" Tony asked.

They all laughed. She didn't find him funny or attractive—not like Peter. She took her seat, and Mr. Thompson came through the door.

"Guys, we have a lot of material to cover for end-of-year tests. Everybody, take your seats. I need your attention on me."

He looked at Penny and smiled. She whispered, "Thank you."

As time passed that day, Penny found herself concentrating

on Peter and nothing else. What was wrong with her? She barely knew the boy, and he was consuming her day. The hours flew by, and before she knew it she found herself at the cemetery next to her parents' tombstones.

"Mom, how am I going to explain Peter to Grandma? She doesn't like the Sampson family. Maybe if she were to meet him, she'd feel different."

She realized how late it was getting and headed home.

CHAPTER 15

Grandma

Grandma was in the kitchen when Penny arrived home. She was cooking something that smelled good. Penny thought she would come right out and tell her about Peter. She hadn't been as angry as she'd thought she would be about her hair. Maybe she would see it the same way.

"Hi, Grandma. What's for dinner? It smells amazing."

"Pork roast. With hot apple pie for dessert."

"How was your day?"

"Penny, is there something you want to talk about?"

"You said when I was ready, I could talk to you about why I suddenly changed my appearance. I want to tell you about a boy I met at school."

"I was pretty sure it had something to do with a boy. Tell me about him."

"Well, he's really cute and smart. He's a senior this year. He seems really nice, Grandma."

"What's his name?"

She had known that was coming. "His name is Peter. I'm pretty sure he's going to college in the fall."

"You two can be good friends."

Phew. She didn't ask me for his last name. So far, I'm in the clear.

They ate in silence, and Penny got up and started cleaning up the dinner dishes. Then it came.

"By the way, Penny, what's Peter's last name?"

"Sampson." She sat back and waited for the bomb to go off. "Does it really matter, Grandma?"

"Did you say what I think you said? Did you say Peter Sampson?"

"Yes, I did," Penny said with more of an attitude than she should have.

"No. No! I forbid you to see that boy."

"Grandma, you don't even know him!"

"You can't see him, Penny!" she yelled.

"I know you hate H.G., Grandma. Peter is not like his father."

"Penny, if you know what's good for you, you will stay away from that boy. All Sampons are alike—no good!"

Penny knew there was no use in fighting with her, so she ran upstairs to her bedroom. She screamed into her pillow and cried herself to sleep.

Morning came too soon. Penny felt as if she hadn't slept much. She went to get into the shower only to find out that she couldn't get out of her room. The door was locked from the outside.

"How could she? I need to get to school!" she screamed.

Penny sat back down on her bed, not believing what her grandmother had done. Just then, she heard her grandma at the door. Her grandma opened it and had a big smile on her face.

"Good morning, Penny. From now on, I am taking you to school, and I will pick you up from the cemetery after school."

"Why are you doing this, Grandma? You have never taken me to school. I've walked every day since Mom and Dad passed away," Penny said, frustrated, thinking she might guilt her into saying she could walk to school.

"I promised your parents I would take care of you when they left that horrible day, and I am not going to break my promise. I should have listened to my inner self that day. It was such bad weather, and I should have told them to stay until the following day. I didn't listen to myself. Today I am going to listen to my inner self. It's saying something is not right with this boy. And I'm listening." She was crying by the time she got done talking to Penny.

"Grandma, it's not your fault. I know you're doing your best." Penny hugged her, and her grandma gave her a big hug back.

"I'd never forgive myself if something were to happen to you, honey."

"I know, Grandma."

"You'd better get ready for school. I'll go get the car warmed up."

Penny started dressing. It was too late to get in the shower. She was upset that she wasn't going to be able to see Peter and especially that she couldn't get a shower that morning. Plus, she didn't want to let her grandma down. She headed downstairs to the kitchen. There was toast on the counter with orange juice in a paper cup. She grabbed both and went out the door. Grandma drove Penny to school in silence. As Penny started getting out of the car, her grandmother grabbed her arm.

"Penny, you know I'm doing this for your own good, right?"

"I know, Grandma." She shut the door and headed up the steps to the front door. Suddenly, she heard her name being called.

"Penny, where were you this morning? I waited in the parking lot until I had to come into school," Peter said.

"My grandma decided she was bringing me to school and picking me up from now on."

"Why the sudden change?"

"To be honest with you, she doesn't want me to see you, Peter."

"What did I do?"

"You didn't do anything. My grandma doesn't like your father."

"Can we talk, Penny? I don't feel like going to classes today."

"You mean skip school? I have never skipped school before. If my grandma finds out, I'm going to be in a lot of trouble."

"You probably don't ever get into too much trouble, do you?"

"I try not to. Ever since my parents died, my grandmother has taken care of me. I don't like to give her much to worry about."

Peter apologized for stepping over the line. "I don't want you to get into trouble. I'm being a bad example. I know all about getting into trouble. I will see you later."

Penny had been about to cave but was happy she hadn't. She went to her first class and made attendance. After the bell rang, she asked for a hall pass. She went to find Peter. She saw him through the window and waved her hall pass at him. He got a hall pass and went to meet Penny.

"I thought about it. Let's get out of here," Penny said.

They walked out the side door and got into Peter's car.

"Where would you like to go?" he said with a big smile on his face.

"Can we go to the cemetery first? I would like to introduce you to my mom and dad."

"Let's go!"

They drove to the cemetery in silence. Penny got out of the car first. She walked over to her parents' gravestone.

"C'mon, Peter. Don't be shy." She giggled. "Mom and Dad, this is Peter Sampson."

"Nice to meet you," he said, and he looked at Penny.

"Can we just sit here a little while?"

"Sure."

They sat in silence for what seemed like a long time. Finally, Peter looked at Penny and asked, "Penny, can I ask you something?"

"You're going to ask me how they died, aren't you?"

"No, I was going to ask you if there were softer seats anywhere around." They both laughed. "Do you want to get something to eat?" Peter's stomach started grumbling.

"Sounds like we'd better."

They walked to the car and drove off.

"Where would you like to eat?" Peter asked.

"Let's go to the food court in the mall. I pretty sure I won't get caught there."

"The mall it is, my lady."

She smiled and sat quietly for the rest of the trip.

They rode the escalator up to the food court. Peter turned around and asked her where she wanted to eat.

"Can we just grab a slice of pizza?"

"Of course."

Pizza was Penny's favorite food. They each got a slice of pizza, and Peter finished his before Penny was halfway done. He told her he was going back for another slice and asked her if she wanted another one.

"I'm not finished with my first piece. No, thanks."

Peter walked up to the counter and turned around, and there she was: Penny's grandmother. She grabbed Penny's arm and dragged her away from the table—of course, not before she called Peter a few choice names. Peter was upset. He was just getting to know Penny and liked her a lot—not just because his father had told him to get to know her. He took his pizza and left.

Penny sat silently in the car while her grandmother yelled at her. Instead of taking Penny back to school, Gracie took her home.

"You need to know why I don't want you to see that boy. When I show you what I must show you, you'll understand why."

They drove into the driveway but didn't park the car in the garage. Gracie opened the garage and told Penny to come inside. She shut the door, knelt, and lifted a piece of carpet. She opened a door in the garage floor that Penny hadn't known existed until now. She walked down the steps into a room under the garage. Gracie walked to a stack of boxes. She handed Penny a piece of paper that appeared to be a birth certificate.

Penny read it: "Gracie Ann Sampson, born January 9,

1959." She looked up at her grandmother and asked how that was possible. "You and H.G. are brother and sister?"

"No, he's my half-brother. Peter Sampson, H.G.'s father, had an affair with my mother. He sent her away and told him if she kept the secret, I would never want for anything. I didn't know anything about it until my mother got sick. She showed me my birth certificate. My adopted father's name was Winchester. I kept his name even after I found out that my real name was Sampson. Well, legally, it was Sampson. My so-called adopted father never adopted me. They just used his last name. My mother had cancer and knew she didn't have much longer. She told me the story, and it wasn't until I met H.G. when he was trying to get out of trouble that, she told me about him. She begged me not to say a word to anyone. The money she got from Peter Sampson's will would have to be returned if I told. The money was helping my mother with her cancer treatments. I kept her secret until now."

Penny felt defeated. She was Peter's cousin, and she couldn't tell him why she couldn't see him anymore. "Let's move away, Grandma. There is nothing keeping us here. Please!"

"I thought about moving when your grandfather died, but I didn't want to leave you and your parents. Then the accident happened, and I didn't want to take you away from what you knew. Now we can sell the house and move."

"Grandma, why didn't you tell me when I told you who I liked?"

"I wasn't going to keep you in the dark for too long, Penny. I just had to find the right time to tell you. I was going to tell you after school today, but then the school called to let me know you were absent, and I knew what you had done. I never dreamed you would disobey me. I knew I should look for you in the cemetery. When I got there and you weren't there, I thought about another place you would go without me finding you. I'm glad you're predictable. Pizza—really, Penny?" She giggled a little. "Anyway, I spoke to a realtor today. I thought we could go somewhere near the beach. I know you always loved going to the beach with your mom and dad. I also know it's your junior year. If you want, we can leave after school lets out, and you can start your senior year someplace warm."

"As long as we get far away from the Sampons," Penny said.

"That's another thing I wanted to talk to you about. Don't you find it quite a coincidence that this young boy would talk to you the day after H.G. was here?"

Penny hadn't given it much thought until then. "Oh my gosh, Grandma, you're right. He was playing me all along! I hate him! I hate Peter Sampson! I'd like to leave as soon as school is over for the year. I will stay away from him, Grandma. I promise. I feel like such an idiot."

"Don't blame yourself, sweetheart. You got caught up in an unfortunate situation. I'm sorry."

"You don't have anything to be sorry about, Grandma. I think I'm going to go to the cemetery. I will see you for dinner."

"Do you want a ride?"

"No, I need the fresh air. I'll walk. See you for dinner."

Penny walked to the cemetery. Peter was sitting next to her parents' gravestone.

"Get away from me, Peter Sampson!" she screamed.

"What did I do?"

"You know very well what you've done. I'm not going to let you make a fool out of me again! Get out of here!"

"You can't tell me what to do. Maybe you could explain to me why you're acting like this!"

"Your father put you up to this—you and me—didn't he?"

Peter looked at the ground. "Yes, he did. But I have gotten to know you, and I like you, Penny." He spoke while still looking at the ground.

She looked away and said, "I don't want to spend any more time with a liar! I can't spend any more time with you, Peter."

"I know my intentions were not true in the beginning, but I really do like you, Penny."

"You don't understand, Peter. We can never be together!" She didn't want to give the reason away, but she couldn't stand to look at the sadness on Peter's face.

"Why? Tell me why I can't see you!"

"Because we are related!"

"What? What do you mean we are related?"

"Your dad and my grandmother are half brother and sister."

"That's not possible. My grandfather couldn't have girls. Every time Grandma would get pregnant with a girl, she lost it."

"Well, your grandfather had an affair with my grandma's mom. She had a girl: Gracie Ann Sampson."

"Penny, that's not possible. My grandfather had a vasectomy after my father was born. I heard my parents arguing one night before Edie was born. Mom was complaining about having a girl and telling my father he was just like his dad, never wanting a girl in their family. If he didn't want a girl, he should have gotten a vasectomy like his father did after he was born. We can't be related, Penny. My grandfather never had any more kids after my dad was born."

"Peter, your grandfather had an affair with my grandma's mom. He has a girl."

"When was your grandmother born?"

"January 9, 1959."

"Penny, my dad was born in 1958. There is no way my dad is your grandma's half-brother. If it helps, I will get it out of the horse's mouth. I will ask my father."

Penny was scared now. Her grandma had told her not to tell anyone. Two times in one day, she had disobeyed her grandma.

Peter sped away.

Penny looked down at the gravestone. "Mom and Dad, what kind of mess have I gotten myself into?"

CHAPTER 16

Gracie

Peter drove home as fast as he could. He wanted answers. What kind of man would ask his son to get to know someone he could possibly have feelings for and not let them know they were related? His father's car was in the driveway when he pulled in. He ran up the steps and into the foyer.

"Dad, where are you? Dad!"

His father walked out of his study. "What the hell is all this yelling? I was on an important business call."

"We need to talk, Dad." He looked at Cindy. "Privately."

"Come in here then." He pointed to his study.

As soon as H.G. shut the door, Peter started yelling. "Why didn't you tell me that Penny's grandmother is your half-sister? That means Penny is my cousin! What the hell kind of man are you?"

"You'd better calm it down, young man. Who told you this nonsense?"

"Penny's grandmother showed her the birth certificate. Her name is Gracie Sampson!" Peter yelled.

"First thing, Peter, you have no clue what you're talking about. Next time you come into the house yelling like a fool, you'd better find out the entire story before you call me names. Second thing, Gracie Haul is no Sampson. You must not think too highly of your father, Peter.

"Emily Winchester is Gracie's mom. She was your grandmother's best friend. At the time Emily was pregnant with Gracie, Gracie's father-to-be was a son of a bitch. He used to beat the crap out of Emily. Emily told Henry Watkins that Gracie was my grandfather's baby so he would leave her. My father—your grandfather—told Emily he would take care of Gracie. My grandmother knew all about it. My father had a vasectomy after I was born. So, you see, there is no way my father could be Gracie's dad. His name is on the birth certificate so that Henry couldn't come back and take Gracie. They lived with my parents up until she met that Winchester man. Your father might be a lot of things, but I'm not a sicko." H.G. thought, *if only she were my half-sister, I would have possessed the locket a long time ago.*

"Do you have proof, Dad?"

"Yes, I have a signed affidavit stating that Henry is the real father of Gracie and that my father was an adoptive father. There was money involved. So, my parents covered all their bases."

"How am I going to explain this to Penny?"

H.G. looked at Peter. "You're not going to. You're going to let her think that you're cousins. Gracie Haul has something of mine, and I want it back. You're going to help me get it," H.G. said with conviction.

"No, I'm not. I won't be a part of whatever it is you and Penny's grandmother have going on. Why can't you act like a human being and ask her for it, Dad?"

"I have been down that route. She refuses to hand it over. It belongs in our family."

"What is it?" Peter didn't really think he was going to get an answer.

"It's a piece of jewelry. It's a locket. Grandma gave it to Emily as a gift when Gracie was born. When it's given as a gift for a birth, the locket changes loyalty. So, it's in Gracie's family for now." H.G. was looking into space.

"Dad, you act like it's a person and not just a piece of jewelry."

"Peter, again, don't question things you have no idea about. I need that locket. I need Gracie or Penny or whoever has it to give it back to our family. Peter, don't let me down."

Peter was tired of disappointing his father. He told him he wouldn't disappoint him again. He walked out of the study and got into his car. He was hoping to catch Penny at the cemetery, but Penny wasn't there. He resigned himself to talking to her tomorrow. He sat at the cemetery, thinking about his mom. He hoped she would be released before graduation. He also knew he shouldn't have skipped school that day. They were going over term paper grades, and he wanted to know what he'd gotten on his paper. It was another thing that would have to wait until tomorrow.

He drove home and entered the foyer. He overheard his dad talking about getting rid of the Haul women. *That means Penny.* What was he going to do? Peter really liked Penny. He would have to help her somehow, even if it meant disappointing his father once again.

Penny sat in her room, crying. She really liked Peter. How could they be related? It was disgusting. She sat thinking until nightfall. Her grandmother peeked into her bedroom. Penny pretended she was sleeping. Her grandmother left her room, and Penny decided she was going to sneak out. She needed to talk to Peter. She needed to find out what Peter knew. She called Peter and asked him if he could meet her in the cemetery. He told her he had some good news and said they could talk when he met her.

He was waiting in the cemetery next to her parents' gravestone when she got there. "Do you want to go sit in the car, where it's warmer?" he asked.

"Sure." She followed him to his car, dying to hear about what he had learned.

"There is no way we are related, Penny. My father told me all about your grandmother's mom. She was my grandmother's best friend. Gracie—your grandma—was born to a Henry Watkins. He was a very cruel man, so my grandfather told her to put his name on her birth certificate. That way, Henry wouldn't have anything to do with your grandma's mom. My dad has proof. I also found out why he is so interested in your grandmother. She has a locket that belongs to the Sampson family. He said his mother accidently gave it to your grandmother's mother as a gift when Gracie was born. The locket would have been my father's if she hadn't given it away. It changed loyalty when your grandmother received it. So, you see, we can't be related, or the locket would have gone to my father through family inheritance. Now it belongs to your grandmother's family line. You'll be the next person to get the locket. If it had stayed in the Sampson family, I would have gotten the locket after my father. Do you understand now?"

"I'm so happy, Peter." She gave him a big hug.

"There is something I need to tell you. My father is not going to stop until he gets the locket. I overheard him talking to someone on the phone when I got home. He was saying something about you and your grandma. How he needed to figure out a way to stop you. Penny, you and your grandma are in danger. You need to figure out a way to keep yourselves safe." Peter looked at Penny and thought, *I could spend the rest of my life with this girl.*

Penny looked up at Peter, and he leaned over and tried to kiss her. She moved away. She had never been kissed before.

"What did I do?"

"You didn't do anything, Peter. I have never been kissed before."

"So, you pucker your lips, and we touch each other with our mouths," he said with a little giggle.

He got closer. This time, Penny closed her eyes and let Peter kiss her. She thought she felt butterflies in her stomach. She wasn't sure, so she leaned in and kissed him harder. Yep, those were butterflies. She liked kissing Peter. However, she knew it was getting late, and her grandmother would probably check in on her one more time.

"As much as I would like to stay here all night and kiss you, I had better get back home. If my grandmother catches me out, there will be hell to pay," Penny said.

"At least let me give you a ride home. I will drop you off down the road from your grandma's house, so you won't have to walk that far." Peter was guiding her to his car.

"Okay, you win!" They giggled together.

She snuck in the back door as quietly as possible, but the damn dogs started barking. Grandma came around the corner.

"Where are you going, young lady?" Grandma asked.

Penny thought to herself, *she thinks I'm going out the door.* "I was going to walk to the cemetery to talk to Mom and Dad."

"You'd better wait until tomorrow. It's getting late, and you have school in the morning."

"You're right. I am still a little tired. Good night, Grandma," Penny said, and she leaned in to kiss Gracie on the cheek.

"Good night, sweetheart."

Penny walked up the steps two at a time. She was happy her grandmother hadn't caught her going out, and she was even happier that she wasn't related to Peter. She wondered why her grandmother hadn't mentioned anything about moving. Maybe she wouldn't take her to school in the morning either. She fell asleep after she showered.

That night, she dreamed about Peter. The dream was vivid. Peter was in the kitchen, yelling at her grandmother, telling her the locket belonged to his family, and she needed to give it back, or else she was going to end up dead. Penny woke up abruptly with sweat rolling down her face. What was she going to do? How was she going to help her grandma get away from H.G.? Peter would help them. At least she thought he would. She fell back asleep.

The sun was shining through the window when she woke up for the second time. She knew it was late. Her alarm hadn't gone off. She looked at the clock near her bed. It was 9:00 a.m.

Penny jumped out of bed and ran downstairs. She called out to her grandmother but didn't hear anything. The dogs started barking

"Dusty, Rumor, shut up!"

She ran back upstairs to see if her grandmother had slept in. She wasn't in her bedroom. Penny went back downstairs and yelled out for her.

"Grandma! Are you here?" Just then, the door flew open.

"Penny, what are you yelling about? Why aren't you in school?"

"I overslept. I thought you were taking me to school," Penny said as she yawned.

"I guess I have to today. I don't think I need to take you to school anymore."

Penny was happy to hear that. She ran upstairs and got dressed for school, thinking about Peter. He was probably wondering where she was that morning, especially after last night. She needed to talk to him. She needed his help. They had to keep her grandmother safe. It was ten o'clock when she finally made it to school. Before she got out of the car, her grandmother told her she was seeing a realtor that day. She was going to put the house on the market, and they could leave after school let out.

"Can we talk about this later, Grandma? I have to get to class."

Her grandma gave her a hug goodbye. "I'll see you when you get home."

"Are you picking me up from the cemetery?" Penny asked, holding her breath.

"No, I don't think it's necessary anymore. See you later!"

Penny walked into school and signed in at the office. She got through her classes and found Peter at the end of the day.

"Where were you this morning?" he asked.

"I slept in. I guess I was really tired; I never do that."

They walked to his car, and both got in. They didn't talk until they got to the cemetery.

"Peter, I need your help. We need to keep Grandma safe. What am I going to do?" Penny said with a frown.

"Are there any relatives you could go live with? My father is not going to stop until he gets what he wants," Peter said.

"I don't think there is anyone. My grandfather died and then my parents. Now there's no one left. We don't have any relatives. What am I going to do? And Grandma wants to move to the beach at the end of the school year. I don't want to leave you."

"We need to get that locket. She is in danger if she has it. You need to find out what is so important about that locket. There must be something about it—that is why my father wants it. Penny, we need to keep your grandma safe."

They drove until they got to a house near Penny's grandma's, and Peter let her out. "I will see you tonight."

Penny walked the rest of the way home. Her grandmother was in the yard, cleaning up.

"Hi, Grandma!"

"Hi, honey. How was your day?" Gracie asked, looking up at her from her plants.

"Good. Can we go inside to talk?"

"Sure, I will be right in."

Penny walked inside. Dusty and Rumor started wagging their tails. They knew Penny would give them a treat. She had to remember to take some treats for later when she got back inside the house after being with Peter in the cemetery. She took her stuff up to her room and put it away. She walked downstairs and headed for the kitchen. She grabbed a snack, and her grandmother came through the back door.

"What's up, sweetie?" Gracie asked.

"I've been thinking a lot about the Sampsons lately. Why would H.G. want a piece of jewelry? What is so special about the locket that he would be so cruel to you to try to get it?" Penny said, hoping her grandmother would give her the answers she was looking for.

"Why are you asking now?" Gracie said with a funny look on her face.

"I've been thinking a lot about it since the whole Peter incident. I'm just curious."

"I guess now is a good time for you to learn about it. Follow me," Gracie said.

They went into the garage and down into the room under the garage floor.

"These books will tell you what you need to know about the locket. If you want, you can read them."

"Grandma, does the locket have special powers or something?"

Gracie gave her a sideways glance. "What's the 'or something' you're talking about?"

"I mean, if you wanted to hide away, does the locket help you in some way?"

"Yes, it does. You must read about it. If I told you everything, we would be here for an entire month."

Penny looked down at the floor. "Can I read about that part of the locket?"

"You can, but why are you so interested in that part?" Gracie asked with one eyebrow raised.

"I was thinking if we had to leave in a hurry, we could go into the locket."

"Well, you don't have to worry about that. We don't have to leave."

"Can I read about it?" Penny asked.

"It's in book number four," Gracie told her.

Penny grabbed the book and headed for her bedroom. She couldn't wait to tell Peter about what she'd found. They ate dinner, and Penny told her grandma she had a lot of homework to do. She was going to wait until later in the evening to sneak out. It was getting toward the end of the year, and she had to catch up on some of her homework in order to pass her classes.

She called Peter to let him know it wouldn't be until later that she would meet him at the cemetery. He said that was fine and promised he would be there. She finished her homework and started reading a little about going inside the locket. She was so excited she could hardly wait for her grandma to go to bed. She heard the shower running and decided it was almost time to leave. As soon as her grandmother checked in on her for the night, she would sneak out.

CHAPTER 17

It's Gone

Penny headed for the cemetery and thought she saw headlights. She did. Peter was waiting for her when she got there.

"Peter, I know how we can help my grandmother. I learned a lot about the locket. The one thing we can do is hide her inside. Now I know why your father wants it so bad. It does have a lot of powers. I'm not sure what all it does, but my grandma has several books about it."

Penny was talking so fast Peter could barely keep up with her. "You mean we can get her inside the locket? That's a great idea. Just until Dad thinks she left and is not coming back."

"Peter, I want you to come home with me and explain everything to my grandma. The relationship between your dad and her. How he wants her dead."

"Wait. I didn't say he wanted her dead. I just said he wants her gone. I'm not sure what that means, but wanting her dead is harsh." Peter looked away. He hadn't thought about what wanting her gone meant.

Penny knew. She knew about the locket now, and she was going to be in danger.

"Maybe we should wait until after school tomorrow to tell her. She might be angrier with you for being out this late. I don't want to give your grandma any more reason to hate me," Peter said, looking at the ground.

"We can't wait until tomorrow. If your father is planning something, the sooner the better."

They got into the car and drove to Penny's grandma's house. When they pulled into the driveway, the dogs started barking. Gracie came out of the house with her gun. Penny got out of the car first.

"What in the name of all things under the sun are you doing with that boy? I thought you went to bed."

"I know, Grandma, but you really need to listen to what Peter has to say. Please. For me?"

"He's got fifteen minutes. If I don't like what he has to say, I'm calling the cops."

Penny and Peter followed Gracie inside the house.

Peter cleared his throat and then started speaking. "The locket is loyal to you because you're not a Sampson."

The statement caught Gracie's attention. "How do you know anything about that?" she asked.

"My father told me the story of your mother, Emily Winchester. My grandmother gave her the locket as a gift to you when you were born. If you were a real Sampson, the locket would have been passed to my father. It stays in the family line, so to speak. Your father was a real son of a bitch. I hate to be the one to tell you. He never knew you existed. They—my grandparents—kept you away from him by claiming you as a daughter. Until your mother married Paul Winchester. I guess he knew the story. He decided he was going to bring you up as his own. They never legally changed your name, or Henry Watkins, your real dad, would have found out. So, you see, we are not related."

It was a lot for Gracie to take in, and she fell into a chair.

"My father wants that locket. He is not going to stop until he gets it. Penny and I think we could hide you away until it's safe. Just long enough for my father to think you left and are not coming back. He will quit looking for you eventually. He might get some private eye to look for you, but who would ever think you went inside a locket?"

"What about my granddaughter? Who is going to take care of her?"

"I will keep her safe," Peter said.

"There are things I have to do before I can leave. It's going to be a couple days." Gracie started pacing back and forth through the living room as she spoke.

"You don't have a couple days. I heard my father say he was going to take care of you this weekend."

"I have to make sure Penny has everything she needs. I can't leave until then. If you want to help us, Peter, you need to give me at least until tomorrow night. You also must promise me that nothing will happen to my granddaughter. Penny, your eighteenth birthday is tomorrow. You can stay on your own. You're going to have to tell people I went away, and you're not sure where I went or when I'm going to be home."

"I will be okay, Grandma." Penny hugged her grandmother.

"Penny, I need to know you are going to be safe."

Peter said, "I will be here tomorrow night. Penny, you will have to read up on how this is going to work. I will keep an eye on my father until we meet. I'll let you know where he is and what he's doing. I promise you I will take care of Penny. I won't let anything or anyone harm her. I need to get home before my father starts asking too many questions about where I've been. I'll see you in the morning, Penny. Gracie, I will be here tomorrow night." Peter walked out of the house, and Gracie looked at Penny.

"Do you trust him?"

"He has told me the truth about everything, Grandma. Even the part about his father putting him up to getting to know me at first. I think we can trust him."

"All right, sweetheart. Why don't you try to get some sleep? We have a big day tomorrow."

"Good night, Grandma. I love you."

It was the first time Gracie had heard that in a while. They both walked upstairs and went into their rooms. Penny thought about sleep but knew she had too much to read. It was midnight when she closed book number four. She also made sure her alarm was set. Sleep came quickly.

It seemed it was morning as soon as she laid her head on the pillow. Penny went downstairs to meet her grandmother for breakfast, but she wasn't there. She had left a note for Penny:

> Penny, I need to speak to Mr. Smith at the bank this morning and run some extra errands before I leave. I will see you after school. Love, Grandma

Penny was a little disappointed she didn't get to have breakfast with her grandmother, but she knew she had to get used to
being alone. She ate her toast and drank her orange juice. She
went upstairs to take a shower and get ready for school.

Peter was in the parking lot when she arrived at school.
"Penny, did you find everything you need for tonight?" he asked.

"Yes, but I'm worried about Grandma. I'm not sure she's
ready to be gone without having a plan to come back. I don't
know. Maybe it's just me."

"Everything will go as planned, and we will get her back as
soon as possible. My father is going out of town for a few days.
That will give us a little more time if she needs it. But I think
we'd better do this. The sooner the better."

They walked into school quietly and then said their goodbyes until the end of the day. The day seemed as if it were going
backward. Time felt as if it were standing still.

Penny thought, *I need to get home to talk to Grandma. I think
I will just skip the cemetery today.*

Grandma's car was in the driveway. Penny was happy to see
that she was home. She needed to go over the spell with her and
let her know that H.G. was out of town. If she wasn't ready to
go that night, she could wait a day.

"Hi, Grandma. How did you make out with your errands
today?"

"Good, Penny. I went to the bank and took out a few thou-
sand dollars for you. I left instructions in my drawer next to my
bed, including different passwords if you need more money. I
hope I'm not gone too long, but if I am, you will be taken care
of financially. There's another thing I want to go over with
you, Penny. I want you to place the locket with your parents at

the cemetery. There is a compartment on the bottom of their gravestone, and I have a few items inside it. I want you to put the locket in there. I also want you to promise me you'll do it alone. I don't want Peter to know about the compartment. Promise me you'll do that for me."

"I promise, Grandma," Penny said.

"Did you get a chance to read through the instructions for placing me in the locket?"

"I did. Grandma, if you're not ready and you want to hold off a day, I know H.G. is gone for a few days, so you don't have to leave tonight."

"That's very convenient of him. Being out of town when I'm gone."

"Grandma, he doesn't know you're going anywhere."

"Let's hope he doesn't. Penny, take this." She handed her a cross she had worn around her neck since Penny was a little girl. "This will open the drawer next to my bed. Remember, if you need anything else, go inside the drawer and get it."

"Grandma, I didn't read about how I was going to bring you back home. Can I do that before dinner?" Penny asked anxiously.

"Let me go get book number five. It will give you specific instructions on how to return your loved one."

Gracie went to the garage to get the book for Penny. When she got back, she asked Penny again if she trusted Peter.

"I do, Grandma. Let me take this up to my room, where it's quiet, and I can concentrate."

Penny carried the notebook upstairs, lay down on her bed, and started reading. She came back down after a couple hours and looked for her grandma. She was in the kitchen, getting dinner ready.

"Grandma, are you sure you want to do this? I understand how to bring you back, but what if something happens to me? You'll be stuck in the locket for good."

"Penny, I have an alternative way of escaping. I don't think I will wait for too long for you to bring me back. I don't care if H.G. finds me. He will wish he hadn't. Instead of me leaving, maybe we should get rid of him." Gracie giggled a little.

"That would be ideal, but I'm afraid too many people would be looking for him."

"Yes, you're probably right. What time is Peter going to be here?" Gracie asked.

"He said after he eats dinner," Penny said. "Let's sit down and finish our last supper."

They ate in silence. When they'd finished, there was a knock on the door. Rumor and Dusty started growling.

"Quiet, boys. It's just Peter."

Penny opened the door, and Peter was standing there. "We are just finishing dinner," she said. "I'm going to clean the dishes, and then I guess we will be ready."

When the kitchen was clean, they all gathered in the living room. Gracie shut the curtains.

"Okay, Penny, all you have to do is read the commands. I love you, sweetie."

"I love you too, Grandma."

Penny opened the locket and read the following: "Come into the locket, Gracie Haul, where you will reside on the other side until you're called back again."

Suddenly, Gracie's body dissolved into dust and swirled

into the locket. Penny shut the locket and looked at Peter. "It's done."

Peter looked at Penny, gave her a hug, and vowed he would be there for her.

"Peter, can I be alone right now? I need some time to myself so I can try to get used to all of this."

"Okay, do you want me to call you later?"

"That would be great."

Peter headed for the door, and Rumor and Dusty growled at him.

"Boys, keep still," Penny said. "Don't worry; she'll be back soon."

Penny looked out the window to make sure Peter was gone. Then she took her grandma's car keys and drove to the cemetery. She walked up to the tombstone and reached down to find the button that opened the secret compartment. It was dark, so she turned her phone's flashlight on so she could see. She saw a few things but decided to leave them alone. She placed the locket in the compartment.

"See you soon, Grandma."

She hit the button, and the compartment door closed. She didn't realize that Peter was watching her from a distance. She got up and left for home.

Peter went over to the gravestone and opened the compartment, as Penny had just done. He felt horrible, but he needed to keep Penny safe. He grabbed the locket and drove home to his father.

Penny arrived home, and a sadness came over her. She hadn't felt that way since her parents had passed away. She thought, *don't be silly, Penny. Grandma will be back.* She went inside, and the dogs started barking and growling at her. She told them to be quiet. They lay down and started whining. "Don't worry, boys. She'll be home soon."

She went upstairs and placed the cross in her jewelry box. Then she hopped in the shower and got ready for bed. She was going to call Peter, but she didn't feel like talking to him right now. She got into bed and fell asleep.

Penny woke up feeling sad. She missed her grandmother. She went downstairs and made breakfast. There was a knock on the door. Mrs. Harper, the next-door neighbor, had come calling for her grandmother. She opened the door to questions about where her grandma had gone.

"Mrs. Harper, good morning."

"Is your grandma here?"

"No, she never came home last night," Penny lied.

"That's funny. I saw her car pull into the driveway late last night. She was supposed to make cookies for the ladies' auxiliary today. Are you sure she isn't home?"

"I will let her know you stopped by when I see her, Mrs. Harper. Have a good day."

She didn't feel like answering any more questions about her grandmother's whereabouts. *This is not going to be easy.* Suddenly, the phone rang. It was Detective Knapp.

"Penny, is your grandmother home?"

"No, she's not. Can I take a message?"

"Just let your grandma know we are doing a safety check on her. It's about her trip to the bank yesterday."

"As soon as I see her, I will let her know to give you a call. Goodbye, Detective."

Things were not going as planned. This was going to be

harder than she had originally thought. *I need to speak to Peter about this to tie up loose ends*, she thought. Then she remembered that her grandmother had taken a large sum of money out of the bank. *That's what the police are calling about.* How was she going to get around this one? *Peter had better get here soon.*

She waited until after lunch for Peter to arrive. He never showed up. She tried calling him, but his phone went right to voice mail. She tried texting him, but she could tell he wasn't getting any texts. *What is going on? Maybe this wasn't such a good idea after all.* She would have to think of another way to keep her grandma safe.

She hopped into the car and drove to the cemetery. She went right to her parents' gravestone and opened the compartment on the side of the grave. She looked inside.

The locket was gone.

Who could have taken it?

"Peter Sampson, I hate you!" she screamed.

He must have been there last night when she put the locket away. She couldn't believe he would do such a thing. She'd trusted him. *Grandma was right! He's a snake!* How was she going to get her grandmother back now? She started crying while she walked back to her car.

When she arrived back home, she had tears rolling down her face, but then she spotted the patrol car. It was Detective Knapp. Penny parked the car and slowly got out.

"Where is your grandmother, Penny? I knocked on the door several times, and there was no answer."

"Detective, I don't know where she is. She was home this morning," Penny said as she looked at the ground.

"That's funny. When I spoke to Mrs. Harper, she told me

she asked you this morning where your grandmother was, and you told her she didn't come home last night. Do you mind if I go inside and look around?"

"Not at all. Come on in." She led him into the house. Dusty and Rumor started growling at her.

"Those your dogs?"

"No, they're Grandma's."

Detective Knapp looked around the living room and then went into the kitchen. On the counter was a knife. It had blood on it.

"Can you explain this to me?"

"No, Detective, I can't. That wasn't here this morning when I left."

"Where did you go?"

"I went to the cemetery to visit my parents."

"Penny, I need you to come down to the station with me for questioning."

"Detective Knapp, I'm telling you. I don't know where that knife came from."

"I'm sorry, Penny, but you're still going to have to come with me."

"Yes, sir."

They got into the patrol car and went to the station. Nothing was going right. She was being hauled away inside a patrol car, her grandmother was stuck in a locket, and Peter had lied to her. What about the knife? How was she going to get out of that one? She sat outside Detective Knapp's office and started crying. She would just have to tell him the truth.

He couldn't make heads or tails out of her story. It wasn't

until she mentioned Peter Sampson that Detective Knapp started to pay closer attention.

"So, what you're saying is, your grandmother is stuck inside a locket that originally belonged to the Sampson family, but your grandmother's mother received it as a gift when she had your grandmother?"

"Exactly what I'm saying. Peter took the locket to give it back to his father. My grandmother is inside the locket."

"Penny, you need to wait here. I'll be right back."

He left, and she waited, thinking, *how is he ever going to believe this story?* If she hadn't known it was real, she would have thought she was crazy.

Detective Knapp came back to the office and told Penny she was going to spend some time talking with Dr. Faulk at the BSU. Penny knew she wasn't about to get out of this one, so she agreed to go.

Penny suddenly remembered what her grandmother had told her about the locket having a sister. The sister was good, and it was a watch. She also remembered that Katie O'Reilly worked at the BSU. Katie could help her, she hoped.

CHAPTER 18

~

She Knows about the Watch

Katie had seen Penny around school. She always looked disheveled and dirty. She had dreadlocks and wore the same clothes a few days in a row before she changed them.

Now Katie was looking at an entirely different girl—the girl she had thought had red eyes when she'd left for home the day Brody died. The girl had asked Cathy if she could talk to Katie. Katie wasn't convinced she should talk to her. She remembered how Papa's watch had felt on her arm the day she had seen her. *Maybe she's like Paula and has more than one personality. Or maybe she's like Tobin and has schizophrenia.* She wasn't sure, but she didn't feel strong enough to dive into a situation that she wasn't fully prepared to help. It took a lot out of her when diseases were involved. *Who am I kidding? I'm not the one who helps them. Only by God's hand are they able to be helped.*

Katie had told Cathy she would see her. Instead of taking her to the children's ward, Cathy took her to the back of the

BSU. They walked down a long hall, she swiped her badge, and they went into another room, one Katie had never been in before. The room had two-way-mirror glass all around it. A guard was sitting outside the room Penny was being held in.

"We have to keep her in here; she is a danger to herself and others. Be careful with her, Katie. I'm not sure how she knows you, but she asked for you by name."

"I know her from school. Well, I don't *know* her know her," Katie said.

"If I see you're having problems with her or Frank hears you call for him, we will be right in to help you."

Katie nodded and asked to be let inside. The only thing in Penny's room was a bed—no desk, no books, and not even a bathroom. There was a sign on the door: High Security. Katie was led into the room, and Penny looked up at her.

"I was wondering if you were going to come see me," Penny said, staring at Katie.

Papa's watch wasn't burning her arm. She was not sure why or what that meant, not unless she had a disease.

"Please sit down, Katie." Penny was pointing to her bed. "I don't have much time to talk to you before they come back in with medicine that puts me to sleep, so could you just hear me out?"

Katie sat down on her bed. "How do you know me?"

"That's not important. What is important is the watch."

Katie looked at her, wide-eyed. How did she know?

"My grandmother told me all about you, your family, and the watch." There was a knock on the door. "Katie, I need you to come back tomorrow. Please! I need your help. It's important for you to know my side of the story. I didn't kill my grandmother."

Katie looked at her in shock. *I didn't know she was in here for killing her grandmother. I can't help her. If her grandmother is dead, there is nothing I can do about it.*

"Please, Katie, it's for your own good. It's about the sister to the watch. Please tell me you'll come back."

"Okay, I will see you tomorrow."

The nurse came in to give Penny a shot.

CHAPTER 19

Peter

Penny woke up from a groggy sleep. She sat at the end of her bed, wondering why Peter had turned on her. She had thought she could trust him. *Grandma knew. She knew how those Sampons are. I was a complete idiot, thinking he liked me. Why didn't I listen to my grandma? Now she's gone, and I'm stuck in here and possibly up on murder charges. Where did that knife come from? How did someone get past the dogs? Peter. It was probably him. But where did the blood come from?* Questions were coming faster and faster in her head. *Banging on the window might help.* "Please let me out of here! My grandmother is not dead! Anybody out there?" She felt defeated. She sat back down on her bed. She was going to go stir crazy. The only thing she could do was look at the four walls.

Just then, there was a knock on her door. Cathy came in to tell her she had a visitor. It was Peter Sampson.

"I don't want to see him!"

"He said you would say that. He also said that it was very important that he sees you. I wouldn't ask you, but he looked desperate."

"I'll give him ten minutes."

Peter walked into the room. As soon as they shut the door, Penny started yelling at him.

"How could you, Peter? I trusted you! I know you took the locket. Where is she? Where is my grandmother?"

Peter looked at the floor as Penny kept yelling. Finally, he spoke. "If you would just be quiet for a minute and listen to me, I will tell you why! I gave up your grandmother for you."

"What do you mean you gave up my grandmother for me?"

"Penny, my father told me he would kill you if I didn't get the locket. But I will get it back. Now that you're in here and safe, I can get it. My father wouldn't dare try to touch you in here. He would be a fool if he tried to come after you in here."

"How are you going to get the locket back from your father? And do you know who placed that bloody knife in my grandma's kitchen?"

Peter looked at the floor again. "I put it in the kitchen. It has animal blood on it. They'll figure that out soon enough and let you out of here. Right now, I need you to stay put. I know you're safe in here."

"I'm sorry, Peter, but I don't trust you. You have my grandmother in that locket, and I'm in here where people think I'm crazy and killed her. Tell me why I should trust you now."

"Penny, I know you don't trust me. I wouldn't trust you if it were the other way around. But I know you're safe now. Once they figure out that it's animal blood on the knife, they will be in here to get you. I need to work fast. I need to visit my mother to find out if she has the combination to the safe in my father's study. I will get the locket back to you. I promise."

Penny hugged Peter and started crying. "They think I'm crazy, Peter. I'm not sure they will let me out. Even if they figure out the knife had animal blood on it, how am I going to explain my grandmother's disappearance?" She laid her head on Peter's shoulder.

"Everything will be okay. You'll see."

There was a knock on the door. "Visiting hours are over for now," the guard said.

"Penny, I will show you that you can trust me. You'll see."

"Peter, just be careful."

He went out the door. Penny felt a sense of relief. She was glad to hear the blood wasn't her grandmother's.

CHAPTER 20

Kimberly

Peter drove to the hospital to see his mother. He felt bad he hadn't seen her since she was admitted. He wasn't sure how he felt about her. Tommy was still afraid of her. Edith missed her but didn't miss her drinking. Tony was oblivious. He lived in a fantasy world.

Peter parked his car and went inside. The nurse at registration asked him who he was there to see.

"Kimberly Sampson."

She gave him a funny look. "Are you family?" the nurse asked.

"Yes, I'm her son."

"Follow me."

They walked down a long hall and into another part of the building. Peter had seen a lot of people in hospitals, but there were a lot of people in straitjackets sitting in the hallway, mumbling to themselves. He had never seen anything like that before. They got to the end of the hall and had to go up in an elevator.

The nurse said, "This is where you're on your own. I will swipe my badge, and you'll ride the elevator up to the eighth floor. When the elevator opens, you'll be greeted by a guard. Tell him who you're here to see. They will take you to your mother."

"Thank you."

Peter hopped into the elevator and rode up to the eighth floor. He thought about how to get his mother to tell him the combination to the safe. The elevator stopped. The doors opened, and the guard approached him and frisked him.

"You'll have to hand your car keys over. You can pick them up on your way out. Hang up your jacket over there." He pointed to a closet.

Peter thought that was high security for addicts.

"Who are you here to see?" the guard asked.

"Kimberly Sampson. She is my mother."

"Wait here. I will let them know she has a visitor."

Peter sat on the couch in the waiting area. He looked up and read the serenity prayer, which hung in a frame on the wall: "God, grant me the serenity to accept the things I cannot change, the courage to change the things I can, and the wisdom to know the difference." He thought it was a good prayer not only for his mother but also for himself.

The guard came into the waiting area. "You can come in now."

Peter got up and was escorted to his mother's room. He was a little nervous. He didn't know if his mother wanted to see him. The guard knocked on the door.

"Come in." Kimberly looked up and saw Peter standing in the doorway. "Peter! I'm so glad to see you, honey."

"Wow, Mom, you look great! How are you doing?" Peter said, a little shocked to see his mom looking so good.

"I'm doing really good, sweetie. Looks like I will make it to your graduation."

He gave her a big hug. "I've missed you, Mom. We all have."

She looked at him and raised an eyebrow "Not your dad, though. How's Tommy? I miss him. I feel so horrible about what I did to him. He probably doesn't want me back home."

"He misses you too," Peter lied.

She thought about the night she had thrown the hot water on Tommy. He'd reminded her of Hugh when he called her a no-good drunk. She'd freaked out. There was no excuse for what she had done to her baby, but she hadn't been in her right mind back then. Right now, she was in the best place possible. She was away from Hugh and getting sober. She vowed to be a better mother when she got released. As far as her marriage to Hugh, she would have to see.

"So, Peter, what brings you here to see your crazy mother?"

"Mom, don't say that; you're not crazy. Unfortunately, it was the alcohol. Anyway, I need to ask a favor of you," Peter said, looking embarrassed.

"What is it, sweetheart? There is not much I can do for you in here. Ask away."

"Mom, I need to get something out of Dad's safe in his study. He has something in there that doesn't belong to him, and I need to get it back. Do you have the combination?"

She started laughing. "Peter, you think your father would ever give me the combination to his safe? Honey, I'm not sure we lived in the same house. You know what your father thinks of me. You're not serious, are you?"

"Yes, Mom, I'm very serious."

"I'm sorry, Peter, but I can't help you."

Peter looked defeated.

Kimberly looked at her son and was curious as to why he needed to get inside his father's safe. "Peter, what I do know is that your dad has a painting of his parents in his study, and behind the painting is a lockbox. The keys are hanging under his desk in his study. Maybe you'll find what you're looking for there. Can I ask you what you're after?"

"It's not important, Mom. I must go now. I will be back to see you."

"But you just got here," Kimberly said with some regret.

"I know, but I promise I will come back to see you. Right now, I'm kind of in a hurry."

"Peter, I don't know what you're after, but please be careful, sweetheart. I know your father. If it is something he wants and you go after it, he won't stop until he gets it back. He won't care who he hurts either."

"I'll be careful, Mom. I love you, and I will visit you soon."

Kimberly sat down on her bed. She was afraid for Peter. She knew about the locket. Hugh had come to see her and told her how happy he was about it. She said a prayer for Peter. *When Hugh finds out the locket is missing, he won't be so forgiving.*

Peter drove home as fast as he could. He needed to beat his father home so he had time to look for the locket. He drove into the driveway and didn't see his father's vehicle. He was thankful for that. He tried sneaking inside without bumping into anyone. He walked through the garage and went into the kitchen and down the hallway. Cindy was waiting around the corner.

"Peter Sampson, where have you been? You know you were supposed to be home right after school."

"Cindy, I don't have time to talk to you right now. I'm busy. I have something to do before Dad gets home."

He didn't want Cindy to know he needed to get into his father's study, so he climbed the stairs, watching for her to go into the kitchen.

"You're lucky you made it home before your father got here!" she yelled at him, walking toward the kitchen.

He pretended to walk upstairs but snuck back down and went into his father's study. He went right to the painting. It was hanging right above his father's desk, behind his chair. He pushed the painting to the side and found the lockbox. He then knelt on the floor under his father's desk; the key was hanging there. He grabbed the key and went back to the painting. He unlocked the box, but the locket wasn't inside.

"What am I going to do?"

"For starters, you can tell me what you're looking for."

His father was behind him. *How did he get in here so fast? I just checked the garage, and his car wasn't there.* "Where did you come from?"

"That is none of your concern, young man," Hugh said.

"Who told you I was here? Mom called you, didn't she?"

Hugh gave him an odd look. "What does your mother have to do with you being in my study?"

Peter looked horrified. Maybe his mom hadn't had anything to do with it.

"Next time I stop by the house to pick up my briefcase for a meeting, I damn well better not catch you in my study. Do you understand me?"

"Yes, sir," Peter said with his head down as if he were a dog that had just gotten scolded.

"I want you to make sure your sister and brother are home tonight. Tony has ball practice, but I want you kids in for the evening. Cindy won't be here. I'm putting you in charge."

Peter felt defeated. "Yes, sir, I will be here."

Hugh left, and Peter went to his room.

"How am I going to get the locket? I must go see Penny. Cindy will cover for me."

Peter walked into the kitchen and asked Cindy if she could cover for him that night.

"Absolutely not! Your father left specific instructions that I was to go home and that you were to make sure your brother and sister were home. With the mood that man was in when he left, I wouldn't cover for you even if I could. Plus, I am busy tonight. If you had any brain cells left, you would not defy your father."

Peter knew he'd better stay home. Maybe if he called the BSU, they would let him speak to Penny. He picked up his cell phone, googled the number, and placed the call.

"Good evening. Behavioral Science Unit. Cathy speaking. Can I help you?"

"Hi, Cathy. It's Peter Sampson. Can I talk to Penny Haul?"

"I'm sorry, Peter, but all the patients are eating dinner right now. Try back in a half hour."

"Okay, thank you."

Peter felt some hope. He'd explain to Penny what had

happened. Hopefully she would understand. *I'm trying to help her.*

Cindy called upstairs and announced that dinner was ready. Peter wasn't hungry, so he thought he would get some homework done. He couldn't focus, so he put his book down and started watching TV. He kept looking at the clock. The time seemed to go backward. He lay down and fell asleep.

It was morning when he woke up. How could he have failed to get the locket back? He thought about how disappointed Penny was going to be in him. How was he going to explain this one? *Too late now, Sampson. She'll never believe a word you say,* he thought as he hopped into the shower.

CHAPTER 21

Matthew

Penny was pacing back and forth, watching her feet make patterns in the carpet. *Well, Peter Sampson, you have a lot of explaining to do*, she thought as she traveled back and forth. She was waiting for Katie to get to the BSU. She wouldn't be there until after lunch. *Why do I care about Peter? I can't trust him.* She pictured kissing him. *What's wrong with you, Penny? He has your grandmother in that stupid locket. You can't trust him!* She repeated those words to herself as if trying to convince herself of the fact.

Suddenly, the bell rang for lunch. Penny was hungry because she had skipped breakfast, so she eagerly joined the line to go to the cafeteria. The guard led her down the hall, onto the elevator, and into the cafeteria. She ordered a grilled cheese sandwich and tomato soup. That should fill her up, she thought. Out of the corner of her eye, she caught Katie sitting with a group of nurses. Katie started walking toward her. She wanted to get up, but the guard was watching her. Katie came over to the table she was sitting at.

"Hi, Penny. After lunch, I will have time to sit and talk with you. I've asked Dr. Faulk if we could use his room. So, whenever you're finished, I will take you upstairs. I already cleared it with the nurses and the guard. We can speak in private."

Penny grabbed her plate of half-eaten grilled cheese and a whole bowl of tomato soup and placed them on the counter for the cafeteria staff to clean them. "I'm ready."

Katie led her out of the cafeteria and into the elevator. She swiped her badge and hit the number 2 to go upstairs. The ping announced they were on the second floor.

"Follow me." She led Penny into Dr. Faulk's office. Penny sat on the couch, and Katie sat in a chair next to her.

Penny told Katie everything, including how her grandmother had shown her the locket and how she had put her grandmother into the locket. She also told her Peter Sampson was involved.

"Katie, I wish I never had put my grandmother in that stupid locket."

Just then, Papa's watch started spinning out of control. The hourglass turned upside down, and Penny was back in the kitchen with her grandma. Katie was outside the kitchen door.

"Come inside, Katie," Penny said. "We have to tell Grandma everything before Peter gets here."

Gracie looked at the girls and wanted to know what was going on. Penny hugged her grandmother tightly and told her everything: Peter had taken the locket because H.G. wanted her dead, Detective Knapp had come to the house, and Penny had ended up in the BSU, but Katie had brought her back.

Gracie looked at her granddaughter and hugged her tighter. "I'm so sorry this locket has brought about so much trouble for you, sweetheart. We must come up with another idea. Katie, can you think of how we can get out of this one?"

Someone was at the kitchen door. Katie looked up and couldn't believe who she was looking at. It was the man of her dreams, the one she had run into the night at the restaurant and seen in the SUV. The one she'd followed in her car.

"Can I help you?" Gracie said, opening the door.

"No, I'm here to help you."

"Who are you?" all three said in unison.

"I'm Matthew Morse. Melinda Morse's son. H.G. Sampson's oldest son."

Gracie opened her mouth in shock. "I knew your mother went away before she was to get married to H.G., but I had no idea she had a son."

"Not too many people know about me," Matthew said. "I was born a couple months before Peter. My mother kept up with what was going on with the Sampson's all these years. However, H.G. has no idea about me. Mom passed away last year. I bought the house next to the Sampsons. Before Mom died, she told me about the locket. I know H.G. wants it to use for evil. I won't let him do that. I know it would have been mine eventually if Grandma hadn't given it to your mother when you were born, Gracie."

"So how do you think you can help us?" Gracie asked.

"You can give me the locket, Gracie. I'm sure you've read all the notebooks regarding how to pass the locket on to a rightful heir. I have relations on both sides of the locket. You see, Henry Watkins is my mother's uncle. Your real father."

"How did you know?"

"Peter Sampson Sr. paid my uncle a very large sum of money to stay out of your life. Your mother didn't even know about it. Although the Winchester she married knew about it."

"Is my real father still alive?"

"No, Gracie, he died a couple years before my mother did of pancreatitis. You know he was quite an alcoholic."

Penny and Katie were taking in all this information. Katie was the first to speak.

"How does she know she can trust you? The locket has been used in a lot of bad ways."

"If she doesn't trust me, H.G. will come after both of them and kill them," Matthew said.

"How do you know so much about what he would do?" Katie asked.

"Cindy, their maid, was my mother's best friend. She knows everything that goes on in that family."

Penny suddenly said, "Peter is going to be here soon. We must talk about a plan but not while he's here. I will tell him, Grandma, that you decided to wait another day. Let's get together tonight. You should leave now before he starts asking questions, especially about our having a man around here."

"I need to leave too to get back to work. Penny, Gracie, shall we all meet up tonight?" Katie asked.

"Yes, we will think of a plan and let you two know about it," Penny said.

"Katie, can I give you a ride back to the BSU?" Matthew asked.

"No, my car is just outside. Thank you, though. I will see you later."

Katie couldn't understand why the watch hadn't gone crazy. It wasn't even warm on her arm. Maybe he was the one who would change the locket from evil to good. At least she hoped he was the one. She finally had gotten to meet the man she had been searching for since before her accident. She thought about driving back to the BSU but decided to call her boss and take the day off. She pulled over to the side of the road and called Holly. She told her she had some work to do for school. She wanted to talk to Nana about what was taking place. She wanted to know if Nana knew anything about Melinda and Matthew.

Matthew knew if he could get them to trust him, he would have the locket, and there would be no way for H.G. to get it. He hated H.G. Sampson. He hated what he had done to his mother. He knew the locket had the power to hide individuals or, in H.G.'s case, get someone off a DUI charge. He decided to go to Katie's grandmother's house to ask her for help. He knew a little about the watch and thought maybe if they worked together, they could help each other.

He passed Katie on the road. He had thought she was headed to the BSU, but when she pulled over, he wasn't sure. He drove to the O'Reillys' house and parked his SUV on the opposite side of the road. Then he walked up to the house and rang the doorbell. Teddy started barking and growling. Nana came to the door and opened it just a crack so Matthew could see the dog and wouldn't just come inside.

"Hello, Mrs. O'Reilly. How are you today?"

"I'm doing well. Who are you?"

"Matthew Morse. Melinda's son. I need to talk to you about the watch."

Nana raised her eyebrows. "Did you say you were Melinda Morse's son?"

"Yes, ma'am."

"You're H.G.'s son, aren't you? I asked your mom before she left for Chicago if she was pregnant. How is she doing?"

"She passed away last year."

"I'm sorry to hear that. Come inside, and sit down."

Katie got off the phone with her boss and headed home. Nana's car was in the driveway. She was happy about that. She was so focused on talking to her grandmother that she didn't see the SUV parked alongside the road. Teddy greeted her at the door.

"Nana, where are you?" she yelled.

"In the kitchen, sweetheart."

Katie walked toward the kitchen and spotted him for the second time that day. "What are you doing here?" She looked at Matthew.

"You two know each other?" Nana looked at Katie as if to say, *you didn't tell me.*

Matthew followed Katie to the living room.

"Matthew, what are you really doing here?" she said in a sarcastic manner.

"I was hoping we could help each other. I know about the watch, Katie. Not everything, but my mother told me that the watch was a sister to the locket. I was thinking if we could somehow get the two together, we might be able to get rid of both. That way, life just takes care of itself. People take care of their own destinies, and everyone is safe from the locket and the watch."

Katie looked at him in shock. "You would do that? You

would get rid of the watch and the locket, knowing the watch is good and helps people?"

"Katie, if the watch exists, the locket exists. Don't you see? We would put people's destinies back into their hands."

"I think I'd better talk to Nana about this before I do anything."

Just then, Nana came through the door with coffee. "Here, you two. Have some." They reached out for the coffee, and it spilled on Katie.

"Oh my gosh, that hurts!" She got up to clean the coffee spill, but Nana told her to go change and said she would clean it up.

Katie climbed the stairs and went to the bathroom to change her clothes. When she came back down the stairs, Matthew was gone.

"Where did he go, Nana?"

"He told me he needed to talk to Gracie and Penny Haul. He said he would be back later this afternoon," she said with a grin on her face.

"Nana, don't get any ideas. He is here to explain to you what he wants to do with the watch and the locket."

"What do you mean what he wants to do with the watch? He has nothing to say about the watch. You're the keeper of the watch. What on earth would he, a Sampson, have to say about the watch?"

Katie looked at her and started telling her about his theory of getting rid of the watch and the locket.

"Unfortunately, Katie, that is not going to happen. They tried doing that the year Gracie got H.G. out of trouble. It caused a great earthquake in Pennsylvania. You know we don't get too many earthquakes here. We will all have to come up with another plan to live with the watch and the locket."

Katie knew she was not going to get out of being the keeper of the watch, but what were they going to do to save Gracie and Penny from H.G.?

CHAPTER 22

Again

H.G. was telling Peter that if he didn't get the locket, he wouldn't see his new girlfriend live another day.

"Dad, I will get it tonight. Gracie is going to hide away inside the locket, and you will have it back before you know it."

"Don't let me down, Peter."

"No, sir, I won't."

Peter climbed the stairs and went to his room. How was he going to tell Penny that he needed to keep her safe and that if he didn't get the locket to his father, H.G. was going to kill both? Penny would never believe him. He needed to save her, though, and if it meant she would be angry at him, then so be it. He thought about just taking the locket. He thought about hiding Penny away in the guesthouse so his father wouldn't find her. Eventually, she would have to come out of hiding, though. Then an idea came to his head. He would find a dead animal on the side of the road and plant evidence of Penny killing her grandmother so she would have to be taken into custody. His father wouldn't be able to get to her while she was locked up.

He hopped into the shower and knew he didn't have much time. He needed to go see Penny. He headed for the door, when Cindy came around the corner.

"Where are you headed off to?" Cindy asked.

"I don't have time to talk right now. I need to go see a friend."

"Not before you help me out. I need you to take some stuff out to the guesthouse. Your father has some visitors coming in for the weekend."

"Can't you ask Tony or Edith to help?"

"They're not here; you're the only one who can help, Peter. Tommy isn't in any condition to help yet," she said with a sad look on her face.

"How long is this going to take?"

"About thirty minutes. I won't keep you all day."

She led him to the laundry room and started handing him boxes to take to the guesthouse. He knew he'd better get at it, or he would be there a lot longer than he wanted to be.

CHAPTER 23

~

Cooperation

Matthew pulled into Gracie's driveway. As he approached the front door, he was greeted by Dusty and Rumor. The dogs never barked or growled. Penny was in the kitchen with her grandmother when Matthew knocked on the door. She thought it was weird that the dogs hadn't announced his arrival.

"Hi, Matt. What's going on?" Penny shortened his name and hoped he didn't get mad about it.

"I just came from Katie's house. I think I have a plan to help us all out. I asked Katie if we could destroy the locket and the watch together. I thought I'd run it by you before we all agreed upon it. What do you think? Then H.G. won't have a chance to hurt anyone."

Gracie looked at him. "Matthew, we actually tried doing that a few years back. There is no way of getting rid of them. I thought if you're its rightful heir, you may be able to do something with it. Here. Take it." Gracie handed the locket to Matthew.

As soon as he touched it, the locket's face moved. It was back into the Sampons' family line. He felt the power of the locket immediately. He wasn't sure if that was a good thing or a bad thing. But he knew he was responsible for it now.

Suddenly, Peter was at the door. The dogs started barking and growling at him. Gracie knew he would betray them, so she told Matthew to go into the other room until they got rid of Peter.

"Hi. Let's go outside to talk. Grandma has a visitor," said Penny.

They went outside to the garden area and sat down on a bench.

"Grandma's not ready to leave. We need at least another day."

Peter looked at her, shocked. He knew he had to get the locket and give it to his father. He didn't want anything to happen to Penny. Just then, the door flew open.

"Who is that?" Peter asked.

"Hi, Peter. I'm your half-brother, Matthew!"

Peter looked dumbfounded. "What do you mean my half-brother?"

"I know you're a little confused, but H.G. is my father. My mother and dad were going to get married. Dad cheated on my mom the night of their wedding. Mom found out about it, so we went to Chicago, and I was raised by my mom and my grandparents. Dad doesn't know about me," Matthew said.

"I suppose the locket belongs to you now?" Peter looked at Matthew with relief.

"Yes, I guess you could say that," Matthew said in a voice like his father's.

"When are you going to break the news to Dad? You know he wants that locket. I'm not sure what he'd be willing to do to his firstborn son. Lord knows he's never been happy with me. Does my mom know about you?" Peter thought about her sobriety and feared that hearing about Matthew might set her back to drinking again.

"No, we stayed away from the entire family when Mom and I went to Chicago."

"Can I ask you why you're here now?" Peter said.

"Mom died, and before she did, she told me all about the Sampsons and the locket. She told me it would have been mine if it had stayed in the family. I'm looking at getting rid of it. Maybe you can help me, Peter. Apparently, this locket has helped people who didn't deserve to be helped."

"How do you expect me to get rid of it?" Peter asked.

"We are all going over to meet at the O'Reillys' house later. We can use all the thinking caps we can muster. Do you know about the watch?"

Peter looked at Penny and shook his head.

"I was going to tell you, but I haven't had a chance. The locket has a sister sort of. It's a watch, and it helps people for good rather than evil," Penny said, looking embarrassed that she hadn't had a chance to tell Peter.

"How did you know about it, Matthew?" Peter asked.

"Just call me Matt. My mother was told about the watch when she lived around here. She was told by her grandmother. I never asked her where her grandmother heard about it. I would guess she was friends with Katie's grandpa or grandma. Let's go to Katie's. Maybe with your grandmother and her nana we can come up with a plan."

They all climbed into Matthew's SUV and drove to Katie's house. Matthew knocked on the front door. Penny, Peter, and Gracie followed behind him. Katie came to the door and called for her nana. They entered the living room and sat down. Nana asked them if they wanted anything to drink. Gracie stood up and went to help.

Nana looked at Gracie. "You know we tried this before. Remember what happened the last time?" She raised an eyebrow.

"Naomi, I am aware of what happened the last time. But I found out recently I'm not a true Sampson. Apparently, H.G.'s father was taking care of me because of my alcoholic father. He kept him away from me and my mother."

"I'm sorry, Gracie. I didn't know. Then maybe it will work. Let's get back to the kids. They can usually come up with better ideas than us old farts."

They entered the living room with iced tea for everyone. Matthew was the first one to speak. "What if we try to smash the watch and the locket together? I know you said they couldn't be destroyed, but Katie and I are the true heirs of the two pieces. Should we try it? We could go to the cemetery and use the big stone that sits in the middle. We could take a sledgehammer to them."

Nana looked at Katie. "Are you willing to give up the responsibilities of the watch?"

"Nana, I guess I'm up for letting people take control of their own destinies. But what if it doesn't work? Then what are we going to do about H.G.? He wants to kill Penny and her grandmother."

Gracie said, "Don't worry about me. I'm just worried about Penny. However, now that the locket doesn't belong to us, we need to make sure Matthew is safe."

"You can call me Matt. Peter, you said Dad won't be back in town for a couple days?"

"Yeah, although Cindy informed me, he will have visitors at the guesthouse this weekend. I'm not sure who will be there. Maybe we ought to wait and destroy the locket and the watch after the weekend. Maybe we will need the extra power they provide. I'm not sure what Dad has in mind, but he is adamant that I get that locket back to him. What am I going to tell him? What if he comes after Penny? Or her grandma?" Peter said.

"I will let him know who I am and that the locket now belongs to me," Matthew said.

Katie looked at Matthew. "Are you trying to kill yourself? I don't know about your father, but when it comes to the locket, he has no tolerance. He won't stop until he gets that locket. What he has done to Penny is enough for me to tell you to stay away from him."

"Katie, it's the only way he is going to stay away from Gracie and Penny. I must go see him. Peter, when will he be back?" Matthew asked.

"He said he was going to be gone for a couple days. I don't know when he will be back or whether he'll return at night or in the morning. I think we should wait until we find out what he wants with the locket. I can always try to make a duplicate in shop class. We could pretend to give him the locket. Whatever he's up to, I think the visitors this weekend has something to do with it. He wants me to get it tonight. He was going to call me later this evening."

Matthew looked at the locket. "Do you think you could make a duplicate? That would buy us some time. You can tell him you have the locket, and if he gets home before his visitors, you can give him the fake one to keep him happy."

Peter got up and headed for the door. "I'll be back. I need you to come with me, Penny. You have an eye for detail. Let's get this locket for my father. Matt, I need you to take me to my car."

Gracie stood up. "Well, Naomi, I don't think these kids need our ideas after all. I'm pretty sure they have it all figured out. Come visit me sometime."

"Gracie, you're right. I will come visit soon."

Katie looked at all of them.

Nana spoke up. "Keep us informed, please. I will be waiting to hear from you."

Matthew looked at Katie. "Do you want to grab something to eat?"

"Nana, are you okay with that?"

"Katie, I need to go help at the thrift shop. You go ahead. I will see you later."

They all hopped into Matthew's SUV, and off they went. Gracie got out of the car first. Katie hopped into the front seat. Peter and Penny got into Peter's car.

"See you later, Grandma," Penny said.

Peter pulled out, and Penny waved goodbye to Matthew and Katie.

"Where would you like to eat?" Matthew asked.

Katie wanted pizza and was curious if Matthew remembered she'd worked at the pizza shop. "How about Papa C's? I could go for a slice of pizza," she said, looking at Matthew.

"Do you still work there?"

Katie stared at him. He remembered.

"No, I lost my job there after I got into a car accident. They needed to have a waitress who could work while I was in the hospital," Katie said with a sad look. "Let's go eat."

CHAPTER 24

Papa C's

Matthew and Katie went to Papa C's Pizzeria. He parked out front, and they walked in together. Mary Cello, Papa C's wife, was there to greet them.

"Katie, where have you been? I haven't seen you in months, young lady."

"I'm sorry, Mary. I have been busy with school and working at the hospital."

"Oh, you got that intern position? That's great, honey!" Mary said with excitement.

"Yes, and it has been working out really well, Mary."

"Well, are you going to introduce me to this fine young man?"

"Yes, I'm sorry. This is my friend Matthew."

"Please call me Matt." He held out his hand to shake Mary's, and she pushed it away and gave him a hug.

"Any friend of Katie's is a friend of ours. Nice to meet you, Matt. What can I get you two to eat? It's on the house."

"Mary, you don't have to—"

"Oh, keep quiet, Katie. It's on me."

"Well, Matt, you up for the best pizza in town?" Katie asked.

"Sounds good!"

"What do you like on your pizza?"

Matthew looked at Katie. "You pick."

"Pepperoni okay with you?"

"It's my favorite," Matthew said.

They sat down in the corner booth.

"I'll bring that out to you as soon as it's done," Mary said. "What can I get you two to drink?"

They both said in unison, "Diet Coke." They both giggled and again talked at the same time.

"Thank you, Mary," Katie said.

Matthew looked at Katie and started to say something. Just then, Jamie came around the corner.

"O'Reilly, where have you been, and who is this you're with? I'm Jamie, Katie's best friend. Although you wouldn't know it lately."

"I'm sorry, Jamie. A lot of stuff has been going on. We need a girls' night to catch up." Her eyes darted to Matthew. "This is my friend Matthew Morse. He moved into the house next to the Sampons."

"Is he—"

Katie kicked Jamie's foot.

"Welcome to Pennsylvania. How long have you been here?" Jamie asked, looking at Katie and winking.

"A few months. I travel back and forth to Chicago. That's where I'm originally from."

"Well, I will let you two eat. Girls' night soon?"

"Yes, Jamie, I will call you."

Jamie looked at Matthew and Katie. "See you later, O'Reilly. Bye, Matt!" She left the restaurant.

Matthew turned to Katie. "You know a lot of people in this town."

"I grew up here. My family has been here for ages. So yeah, I guess I do."

"What about your parents?"

"My father died four years ago, and my mother is institutionalized. She couldn't handle life after Dad passed," Katie said with her head down.

"Oh, I'm sorry to hear that."

"Don't be. I love living with my nana. It's been very eventful since I moved in with her, to say the least."

"I bet it has been."

Mary came out with the pizza. "Here you go, kids. Now, eat up. I will go get your drinks." She brought the drinks over and winked at Katie.

"Boy, you weren't kidding when you said it was the best pizza in town. I was going to order one the night I came in here when you were working—the night I helped you with your mop bucket—but the oven was turned off. I should have known it was good pizza if you worked here."

Katie blushed and thanked him. "So why haven't you heard about your father before?"

"I asked Mom about him, but she never wanted to talk about it. He really broke her heart. She never found another man she could trust. I mean, she dated and all. But when a relationship got too serious, she would break it off. Then, when she found out she had cancer, she wanted to make things right. She didn't want me to go through the rest of my life alone. Even though we lived next door to my grandparents, they like to travel a lot. They're both retired professors. So, they're on the road constantly. Or in the air." Matthew chuckled a little.

"I'm sorry about your mom."

"Thanks, Katie."

The rest of the time, they ate in silence. Mary came to the table to check on them. "How was the pizza?"

"Delicious!" they both replied.

"I'm glad Katie isn't keeping this place a secret any longer," Matthew said.

Katie giggled and hit him with her napkin. "I just met you. You can't blame me for not finding this place sooner."

"So, you want me to box the rest of the pizza?" Mary asked.

"Yes, please. I'm sure Nana would like some pizza for dinner. Okay, that was rude of me. Did you want to take it home for later, Matt?"

"No, I'm stuffed. You're going to have to roll me out of here."

Matthew left a tip on the table. They both thanked Mary and said their goodbyes, promising to come back soon. Matthew opened the car door for Katie to get in.

"The next time we go to dinner, you can pick. You did such a good job this time," he said.

"That's awful presumptuous of you, sir. Who says there will be a next time?" she said with a smile on her face.

"I did. Now, get in."

She was still smiling when he hopped in on his side of the car.

"You know I was just kidding out there. Although I would like to take you out again sometime," Matthew said.

"I accept." They both giggled.

"Where to? Should we go back to Gracie's to see if Peter and Penny are back? Hopefully he was able to replicate the locket."

"Absolutely. You took the words right out of my mouth," Katie said, still smiling.

CHAPTER 25

Duplicate

Matt and Katie pulled into Gracie's driveway. Peter's car was parked outside. Matthew walked around his car and let Katie out.

"You ready for this?" Matthew said, looking into Katie's eyes.

"As ready as I'll ever be."

Matthew knocked on the door. This time, Dusty and Rumor barked, announcing that someone was at the door. Penny answered it.

"Come on inside, you two. You must see the locket that Peter made. If I didn't know any better, I would think it really was the real thing."

Matthew took ahold of the two lockets and put them side by side. "Wow, Peter, nice job!"

Peter grinned. "Hey, guys, I know who is coming to the guesthouse this weekend - Pastor Joe Horton and Pete DeSoto. Do you know either of them?

Katie looked shocked. She knew both. She wondered if she should tell them what she knew about both men. She decided she should probably ask Nana if she should reveal what she knew. Maybe she could read in one of the notebooks to see if Papa ever revealed knowledge he gained from the watch. She wondered if Papa ever had disclosed any of his experiences with the watch. That was what she would do. Katie kept quiet. Gracie spoke up.

"I know both. I have heard rumors about them. People in the community think they're outstanding citizens. I've heard different. Yet I don't know what the correlation between H.G. and those men would be. They are both accused of being pedophiles. Pastor Joe likes little boys, and Pete DeSoto likes little girls. H.G. is just into adult women. Why would he want to be associated with those two? Not unless he is looking to blackmail them. Are there any way you kids can find out anything about them? Why they're meeting?"

Peter spoke up. "What if my father finds out he has a fake locket? What are we going to do then?"

"I will introduce myself to him at that point," Matthew said.

Katie shook her head. "No, no, and hell no. Matt, you have no idea what he will do to you. You can't let him know about you yet. Not until we find out what he wants with the locket."

"All right, Katie, I will keep quiet for now. Sooner or later, I'm going to have to reveal myself to my father."

Katie didn't like that at all. She knew H.G. was dangerous. She knew if he found out he had a faulty locket; he would go crazy. "Peter, he won't know that he doesn't have the real locket. He'll just think he doesn't have the power to control it, and he might come looking for you, seeing as you're the next in line to receive the locket. Or so he thinks."

Peter agreed. "Well, guys, I have to head home. Dad is supposed to call the house phone to see if I got the locket. I have to be there to take the call."

Penny looked at Peter. "Please be careful."

"I will."

Penny gave Peter a hug. "Call me after you hear from your father, please."

Peter nodded and left.

Matthew looked at Gracie and Penny. "Do you trust him to do this without giving anything away?"

Penny looked at Matthew in disbelief. "After what he did this afternoon to make sure your father wouldn't find out about the locket? You're seriously going to ask that question?" She was irritated.

"Penny, I'm only asking this question because my mother told me the Sampsons stick together like glue. I don't want H.G. to figure any of this out. I want him to be just as surprised that the locket doesn't work for him as I was when I found out he was my father."

There was an awkward silence. Katie finally broke the ice.

"I need to get back home to take care of some stuff. Matt, can you give me a ride home?"

"It will cost you." He giggled.

"I guess it all depends on what it will cost for me to get a ride. Maybe I should ask Gracie to give me a ride home."

"Nah, it's just going to cost you a date with me. You can do that, right?"

She grinned at him and then turned to Penny. "You'll give us a call after you hear from Peter?"

Penny nodded. Matthew and Katie walked out the door.

Matthew turned to Katie. "Do you trust him, Katie?"

"I guess I'm going to have to give him the benefit of the doubt. If he proves to be untrustworthy, I will never trust another Sampson again."

"Hey, watch what you're saying."

She laughed. Matthew opened the door for Katie, and she got into the car. They drove back to her house, and the conversation turned again to where they were going to go eat. Matthew pulled into the driveway and spotted a young man hiding behind the tree out front.

"Wait here, Katie. There is someone behind the tree. Let me find out who it is." Matthew walked up to the young man and asked what he wanted.

"Is Katie O'Reilly with you? I need to speak to her. She knew my brother, Brody."

Katie got out of the car and told Matthew she knew who he was and said she needed to talk to him. She would call him a little later. They hugged each other goodbye, and Katie walked inside with Jimmy.

CHAPTER 26

Jimmy

"Please sit down, Jimmy. Can I get you something to drink?" Katie asked.

"No, thank you."

"I'm so sorry about your brother, Jimmy. When did you find out about him? I heard you left for Florida." Katie gave him a sad look.

"I called Mom, and she told me about Brody. She also told me that you were the last person with him. What did he say to you, Katie?"

Katie was staring out the window. "He told me what Pastor Joe did to him. He said he was in love with him, but Pastor Joe didn't want anything to do with Brody anymore. He was heart-broken. He also told me about you, Jimmy. He said Pastor Joe tried to go after you. Is that true?"

Jimmy looked at the floor. "Yeah, he tried to touch me. As you can see, I am a lot bigger than Brody. I can take care of myself. That bastard never touched me again. I should have helped Brody. I knew what that son of a bitch was doing. We should have gone to the cops. Unfortunately, I let it go on for too long. My mother was getting help with rent. She sold Brody to that monster. Now that he's gone, Pastor Joe won't help my mom anymore. She's angry and wants to get back at him. She told him if he didn't pay up, she would go to the cops. I just want them to put that bastard in jail and throw away the key. Can you help me?"

"I'll do everything I can to help you," Katie said. "The one problem we're looking at is that it happened to you a long time ago. We don't have any evidence. However, if you know of anyone else, he went after, we might have a chance to get him."

"I know the boy he has been with recently. I've been watching him since I got back into town. The kid he's messing with now is in the same place Brody was. He has a single mom who needs money. That creep is probably paying his mom off."

Katie looked disgusted. "If you can talk that kid into going to the police, we might have a chance."

"I'm not sure he'll talk. Pastor Joe has him wrapped tightly. Like he did with Brody. At one time, I tried talking Brody into going to the cops, but he kept telling me he loved him."

"Jimmy, I'm so sorry you have to live with this. Brody was innocent. Pastor Joe took full advantage of Brody. Like I said, if you can get this young man to go to the police, we might just have a chance to get this monster. Let me know how you make out. No one should go through what you and your brother went through."

Jimmy thanked her and walked out the door. Just then, Nana pulled into the driveway. She got out of the car with groceries in her hands.

"Who was that young man?"

"Nana, so much has gone on since we talked last." Katie told Nana about Jimmy and Brody, Peter and the duplicate locket, what was taking place that weekend, and H.G.'s visitors. "Nana, I know each of these men. Should I disclose what I know to the group? They have heard rumors about the two. Gracie told us about it. The stories line up with what I know about them. Is there anything in the notebooks that says I can't tell someone what I know about a person the watch has helped?"

"Not to my knowledge, Katie. Although it sounds as if they know plenty about these two guys. Maybe if you tell them what you know, you're confirming the stories. I'm not sure what these men want with H.G., but I know if he is involved, it's no good. Maybe Peter or Matt could plant a listening device of some sort in the guesthouse, and you all can get the story firsthand."

Katie nodded. "That's a brilliant idea, Nana. Then we would have proof that these monsters did what they did. I know that Brody would be here if it weren't for Pastor Joe. Thank God the watch helped Paula out of the situation she was in. I think that if we can get it all on tape, we could take it to the police. Matt lives next door to the guesthouse. We can listen from his house. I need to call him and ask him what he thinks of this idea."

Katie went to get her phone to call Matthew. She had to run the idea by him, talk to Peter and Penny, and try to get some sleep that night. When Matthew picked up the phone, he told Katie he'd be right over. Katie was waiting outside for Matthew. He pulled up and got out of the car.

"Come inside. I have some stuff to talk over with you. Plus, the kid who was here earlier has something to do with Pastor Joe."

Matthew followed Katie into the living room. He sat in the recliner, and Teddy came and sat next to him. Katie thought, *He must be a good soul if Teddy likes him.* "The boy who was here earlier was Brody Benson's brother, Jimmy. I met Brody while I was working at the BSU. He told me things that Pastor Joe did to him that would curl your toes. Jimmy is here to get revenge. He knows what Pastor Joe did to his brother that drove him to his death. The men your father is meeting with are both evil. I know for a fact that Pete DeSoto is a rapist. Before the watch helped one of my clients, he had raped her. They're monsters and need to go to jail. Nana mentioned that you and Peter should plant a listening device in the guesthouse. We could hear them from your place. At least we could find out what those bastards are up to.

Matthew gave her a quick look. "That might work. I guess we'd better get together with Peter and find out when H.G. is supposed to be back. We might be able to ask Cindy for help. She and my mother were very good friends. Let's get everyone together and get this show on the road. I'll call Peter and ask him to meet us at Gracie's house. I can call Cindy too. If anyone knows how to get around the Sampson house, it's Cindy."

"All right, let me tell Nana we're leaving." She went into the kitchen to tell her nana the plan and said they were going back to Gracie's house.

"You two be careful. Let me know how you make out."

"I will see you later, Nana." Katie kissed her grandmother goodbye.

CHAPTER 27

The Plan

Katie and Matthew drove up to the Hauls' driveway and noticed Peter's car was already there.

"I wonder how the call went with his dad. H.G. must think he has the locket by now. Let's find out," Katie said.

Matthew walked to the side of the car and let Katie out.

"Thank you, sir."

He grinned, and they walked to the porch together. Penny and Peter were sitting in the kitchen. Matthew knocked on the door, and Penny came to open it.

"Come on inside, guys. Can I get you something to drink?"

"No, thank you. I'm good," Matthew said.

Katie was thirsty and asked for water.

"Well, Peter, how did it go with Dad?" Matthew asked.

"He's coming home tomorrow night. He's happy that I have the locket," Peter said with a smirk on his face.

"Katie's nana suggested we plant a listening device in the

guesthouse. I thought I would call Cindy and ask her if she could help us."

"Are we sure we want to involve Cindy? I know she would never give anything away, but do we want to put her in that position?" Peter asked, looking a little stunned.

"You're right. It's probably not a good idea. I guess if we must let her in on it, then we will. Do you want to go get something we could use to listen to Dad and his friends?"

Peter nodded.

"We will be back."

Peter and Matthew walked out the door. Katie started telling Penny everything she knew about Pastor Joe and Pete DeSoto. Gracie walked into the kitchen in the middle of the conversation.

"I knew those rumors were true. Those sons of bitches. How could they be such cruel, evil beings? Believe me, I have seen a lot of evil, but when you mess with children, there is nothing in this world that will help you."

"I know, Grandma. I think many people feel the same way."

"I hope you kids know what you're doing. H.G. is a very dangerous man. If he doesn't get what he wants, he brings in some people from the outside who don't care what relationship you have with him. He just has to give the word."

Katie looked at Gracie and Penny. "The only guarantees we have are the watch and the locket. H.G. won't have either." They all laughed together.

"I know we'll have the listening devices, but what are we going to do with them? I mean, the men and H.G.," Penny said.

"I guess we will have to find out what they are up to and go from there, Penny."

"Katie, I'm concerned that when H.G. finds out that the locket doesn't work for him, he may try to hurt Peter."

Gracie spoke up. "Then we will have to get rid of them all. I won't let them hurt you or any of you kids. I will be there with you to give Matt instructions on how to put them into the locket."

Katie and Penny looked at Gracie in shock.

"Grandma, that might be the answer to all of our problems. What if we get rid of all of them? Then there wouldn't be a way H.G. could come after us. Pastor Joe and Pete will be erased from this world and not be able to hurt another child!"

Matthew and Peter returned from the store. Peter said, "We're doing this tonight. After midnight, Dad's security cameras go offline. Each night, they go down for half an hour. Different days, different times. Thursday nights, it's between twelve and twelve thirty. We are going to plant this radio frequency bug behind my great-grandparent's portrait in the guesthouse. We also got this pinhole video camera to hide behind the clock. Look at this. You'd never be able to trace this thing. That way, we can listen and watch what they're up to. Matt and I have to get in and get out fast. We only have that time frame, and then the cameras come back on. We decided we are going to meet up at Matt's house tomorrow night at seven thirty. Penny, I will pick you up, and Matt will pick you up, Katie. That way, we won't have too many cars in the driveway for anyone to ask questions."

"Sounds like you two have this all figured out. Can you take me home, Matt? I have to work in the morning," Katie said.

"Yes, and Penny has school tomorrow," Gracie said. "I think it's time for everyone to get some sleep. You all have a big day tomorrow. But have any of you thought about what you're going to do once you find out what they're up to? Because I have. Matt, I can show you how to put all three of them into the locket. Then all your problems will be solved. They'll never be a threat to anyone again."

"Gracie, as good as that sounds, too many people will be asking about them. If we try it this way and it doesn't work, we might have to try it your way."

They all said their goodbyes and headed for the door. Penny stopped Peter. "Please be safe. I don't want anything to happen to you."

"Don't worry; it won't."

Katie walked out with Matthew and hopped into his car. "Gracie has a good point, you know. If we got rid of them, they wouldn't be able to hurt anyone else."

"Katie, in theory, that sounds awesome. But you know as well as I do that too many people would be asking questions. If we don't get anything on them that we can take to the police, I promise we will try it another way."

Katie sighed. "I'm just worried about you two. I hope you don't get caught."

"If I have to, Katie, I will bring Cindy in and ask her for help."

They pulled into the driveway, and Katie said good night. Matthew leaned over and kissed her on her cheek. "Have a good night."

"You too, and please be careful."

Katie was a little shocked but didn't say anything to him. She walked up to the porch and went inside. Teddy started barking when Katie got home. She put him out the back door.

Nana was there when she shut the door behind her. "Nana, you scared me!"

"I'm sorry, sweetie. How did it go?"

"I guess you could say we are all like James Bond. We are going to spy on them. Hopefully we can get some dirt on them to take to the police. If not, Gracie suggested that Matt put them into the locket. That way, the world would be rid of those evil men."

"That doesn't sound like such a bad idea."

"It doesn't, Nana, but talking Matt into getting rid of them is another thing. He thinks it would cause more problems. People would be asking a lot of questions. You just can't get rid of anyone these days. There are always trails."

"Matt's right. You have a very wealthy man, a pastor of the community, and a restaurant owner. It's not easy for them to just disappear," Nana said.

"We will do everything we can to get information to take to the police. I know for a fact Detective Knapp would love to get H.G. Sampson on something. I'd better get some sleep. I must work in the morning. I love you, Nana."

"Love you too, Sweetheart. If there is anything, I can help you all with, just let me know. Good night, Katie."

Katie climbed the stairs and went to her room. She was so tired she lay on her bed with her clothes on. She fell fast asleep.

Her dream started off in a room full of black-robed men. Each one of them had red eyes. The man at the front of the table was H.G. He was saying something, but Katie couldn't hear what he was talking about. She pressed her head into the room farther to listen, but everything was inaudible. They all started yelling. Just then, one of the guys spotted her. He started walking toward her. She woke up immediately. It was morning.

She jumped into the shower and went downstairs for breakfast. Nana had already left. Katie grabbed some toast and coffee and headed for the BSU. Tammy was at the registration desk when she walked in.

"Hi, Tammy. How are you doing today?"

"I'm good, but you look tired, Katie. Are you sure you want to be here today?"

"I'm good. I just didn't sleep very well last night. I'll catch you later. I have to get upstairs."

"Okay, I will talk to you soon."

Katie swiped her badge and took the elevator to the second floor. Cathy was at the nurses' station when she arrived.

"Hey, Katie, how are you doing? You look tired."

"I'm okay. Did we get anyone new in yet?"

"James is doing an intake on the new girl. But I don't think you'll get to talk with her today. It's been quiet. Although I know better than to use that word. As soon as I do, all hell breaks loose. Dr. Faulk would like to see you this morning. He has your evaluation. He's in the conference room and told me to tell you to go right on in."

Katie walked down the hall and knocked on the conference room door.

"Come in!"

She opened the door and stared at all the people sitting around the table. They all had on white robes. Dr. Faulk told her to come inside and sit down.

"Katie, we have been watching you work. You've done a

great job with the watch. I'm sure you're asking yourself how we know about the watch. Am I right?"

"You could say that," she said with a shaky voice.

"Katie, we are the counselors of the watch. We keep an eye on everything you do. We set you up with the clients we think you can help."

Katie started screaming. "What about Brody? Where were you when I was trying to help Brody? Why didn't you help me? Why?" She screamed it over and over.

She woke up in a sweat. She was still in her dream. She got into the shower and then headed downstairs.

"Good morning, Katie. Would you like some breakfast?"

"No, thank you, Nana. Just a cup of coffee." Katie walked over to the cupboard and grabbed a cup.

Nana took it out of her hand, told her to sit down, and said she would get her coffee. "You look like you didn't get much sleep."

"I didn't. I kept dreaming all night. Not nice dreams either." She thought about calling off work again. She decided she'd better call Cathy to see if she was needed in that day. She picked up her cell phone and dialed the BSU.

"Good morning. Behavioral Science Unit. Cathy speaking. How may I help you?"

"Hi, Cathy. It's Katie. How's it looking today? Do you guys need me to come in?"

"We only have one girl, and James is still doing her intake. But I know Dr. Faulk wants to do your evaluation today. Can you come in after lunch? He's wrapped up in meetings this morning."

"Sure, I'll be in." Katie hung up the phone and thought about her dream. "Okay, Katie, you are going out of your mind."

Nana looked up from her paper. "What did you say?"

"Nothing, Nana." She sat back down at the table and started drinking her coffee. "I don't have to be at work until this afternoon. I think I will run over to the school to see if I have any loose ends that need to be tied up before graduation." She stared out the window.

Nana looked at Katie. "If you need me for anything, I will be at Joyce's house this afternoon. Call me there. I told her I would help her clean out her bedroom closet. Maybe get rid of some of those crazy clothes she has kept forever."

"I will. Thanks, Nana." She finished her coffee and rinsed her cup out. Her cell phone rang.

"Katie, it's Cathy. Can you come in this morning? Dr. Faulk's meetings got canceled, and he wants to give you your review."

"Sure, I'll be right there." She grabbed her briefcase and headed out the door.

Peter was waiting in the parking lot for Penny. Although he'd told her he would give her a ride to school, she'd insisted on walking.

"Good morning, sunshine!" he yelled across the parking lot.

Penny's face went red. "Peter, do you have to do that?" she said, smiling.

"Did you get any sleep last night? You look tired, Penny."

"Not much. I kept having these weird dreams. Did you and Matt get done what you needed to get done?"

"Yes, we are all ready for tonight. Did you want a ride home after school today?"

"I would like to go to the cemetery. So, can you pick me up later?"

"I sure can."

The bell rang, and they walked into school together. People were getting used to seeing them together. The whispering had stopped. Penny assumed they must have moved on to talking about someone else.

Peter gave Penny a kiss on the cheek. "I'll see you after school."

"Okay, see you later." She walked into her first class. Tony Sampson was at her desk.

"You're spending an awful lot of time with my brother lately. You guys like an item or something?"

Penny rolled her eyes. "We haven't talked about being exclusive yet, if that's what you mean. Now, if you'll excuse me, I have to get my books."

"Just be careful with him. You know he's a troublemaker, right?"

"Okay, Tony, thanks for the warning." She liked Peter. She never really had thought about him as a troublemaker, although she didn't know him that well.

The rest of the day went by slowly. She spotted Peter in the parking lot. "Hey, Peter, would you give me a ride home?"

"Of course, hop in. I thought you were going to the cemetery?"

"It was a long night and an even longer day. I'm going to need a nap before we get together tonight." They drove in silence. Penny was just about sleeping when Peter pulled into her driveway.

"You weren't kidding about being tired. I'll pick you up tonight at seven fifteen."

"Okay. See you later, Peter." She walked into the house and went right up to her room and fell asleep.

CHAPTER 28

In Motion

Matthew was pacing back and forth in his living room, waiting for Cindy. He thought he'd better let her know what was going on, especially in case she saw him on the Sampsons' property.

Cindy pulled into the driveway. Matthew was glad she was finally there. She walked up to greet him and told him he'd better hurry with his story. She needed to get to the Sampson house to make breakfast for the kids. Matthew told her what was going on that night and told her about the locket.

"You have the locket?" Cindy asked.

"Let's just say it's back where it belongs."

"I'm worried about you, Matt. What if things don't go as planned?"

"I told you. I will take care of whatever comes along," Matthew said, rolling his eyes.

"That's what I am worried about, young man. You guys

ready for tonight? Do you need me to do anything?" Cindy asked.

"I don't think so. If we need you, we will let you know. Thanks for everything, Cindy."

Cindy walked out of the house and got into her car. She drove up the road to the Sampson house. Edith and Tommy were in the kitchen, waiting for Cindy to get there.

"Okay, kids, what do you want for breakfast this morning?"

"Can we have pancakes?" Tommy said.

Edith looked at Tommy. "You're going to turn into a pancake, Thomas Sampson!" She told Cindy she was just going to have fruit and yogurt that morning.

"Do you two know if your brothers are coming down for breakfast?"

"They already left. They told me to tell you they are going to pick up a doughnut on their way to school and not to worry about them. So, I guess Tommy is the only one eating this morning."

"Thanks for the message, Edith." Cindy started making pancakes, when H.G. walked in the door.

"Daddy!" Edith ran up to her father and gave him a hug. "I've missed you! Can you please quit going away?"

"Edith, I've told you I have to go away for meetings. I brought you and Tommy a gift; it's in my car." Edith went to the car to find her present. "Cindy, can you bring a coffee into my study? I need to talk to you about my visitors tonight."

"I'll be in as soon as I get Tommy's pancakes on the table. They're almost done."

"Thank you, Cindy."

Cindy thought, *He is in a good mood.* She was happy about that. *Things must be going his way.*

CHAPTER 29

Dreams

Katie arrived at the BSU and walked inside. Tammy was on the phone, so she waved to her and headed for the elevator. She thought, *Déjà vu.* She swiped her badge and went upstairs. If Cathy's at the nurses' station, I'm in trouble, she thought. The elevator pinged, and sure enough, Cathy was at the nurses' station. Raymie was sitting with her. Okay, Raymie wasn't in my dream.

"Hi, Katie. How are you?"

"I'm good, Cathy. Is Dr. Faulk ready for me?"

"Let me see."

Raymie was busy on the phone, and Katie was happy she didn't have to make small talk with her. Cathy returned and told her Dr. Faulk would see her. "He's in his office."

It was another win for Katie. They had been in the conference room in her dream. She knocked on his office door and heard him tell her to come in.

"Good morning, Katie. I'm assuming Cathy told you why you're here?"

"Yes, she did, Doctor."

"Well, let's get started."

He went over her review. She couldn't have been happier. She'd received outstanding marks in most areas. Everyone had room for improvement, but for her first time being reviewed, she was happy. She knew that getting such good grades was going to help her with college. "Thank you, Dr. Faulk."

"Thank you, Katie. Keep up the good work."

She left his office and bumped into Cathy.

"So how did it go?" Cathy asked.

"Let's just say I couldn't be happier."

"Katie, you deserve it. You are so good with the patients here."

"Thanks, Cathy. That means a lot to me. Is there anything you need from me this morning?"

"No, go home and celebrate. I will see you on Monday."

"Sounds good. See you Monday."

Katie walked to the elevator, happy to know she had just been dreaming about the BSU. There was no one in a white robe telling her she was doing a good job. No one in the BSU knew about the watch.

She tried calling Matthew, but his phone went right to voice mail. She got off the elevator and looked for Tammy. She wanted to say goodbye to her. She must have been in the bathroom. She walked to her car and tried Matthew's phone again—voice mail. She thought she would go home and take a nap before going out that night.

She pulled into the driveway and saw Matthew's SUV along the side of the road. He started walking toward her.

"Congratulations, Katie. Are you ready to go out and celebrate?"

"Cathy called you, didn't she?"

"I'll never tell. What do you say we go grab a slice of pizza from the best pizza place in town?"

"Matt, I'm really tired. I didn't sleep much last night. Can I take a rain check?"

"Absolutely. Tell you what. I will pick you up at five o'clock, and we will go get something to eat then."

"How about you pick me up at seven so I can take a real nap? We can go eat another day."

"You win!" They both laughed.

"I'll see you at seven. What time is Peter picking Penny up?" Katie asked.

"They said they would meet me at my house at seven thirty. Go take your nap, and I will see you later."

Katie gave Matthew a quick kiss on the cheek.

"You ready for this?" he asked.

"As ready as I will ever be," Katie said, winking at him.

"All right, I will let you sleep for now. But you'd better be ready when I get here."

"Yes, sir!" She smiled, walking into the house. She watched as Matthew drove off.

CHAPTER 30

Working Together

Penny and Peter got to Matthew's house at seven thirty. Katie was listening for any sign from H.G. or his cohorts.

"Hi, guys. Did we miss anything? I know my father arrived home earlier today but went out again. He got back around six o'clock and headed up to his bedroom. Probably taking a shower and getting ready for tonight. He didn't see me leave," Peter said with a smirk.

Matthew asked them all if they wanted some iced tea. Penny and Katie both said yes. He went to the kitchen to get them their drinks. Suddenly, they heard voices, but the video wasn't coming in yet.

Matthew came back from the kitchen with drinks and cheese and crackers. "I thought we could use some snacks for the show."

They heard H.G.'s voice first. "Good evening, gentlemen. We are waiting on two more guests before we begin."

"Did you guys hear what I just heard?" Katie looked around at the group. "Peter, do you know anything about this?"

Penny gave him a puzzled look. Peter shook his head. The video started coming into view. Then Katie saw it: three men in black robes. She felt weak. She looked over, and Penny was dropping to the floor.

"Matthew, what have you done?" Katie said.

"I told you—it's Matt!"

Just then, everything went black for Katie.

"Call Dad, and tell him they're out. We need to get them to the guesthouse," Matthew said.

Peter picked up the phone and called over to the guesthouse. "It's done, Dad. We need Cindy to bring the van over to get them to you."

If Gracie and Naomi find out things aren't going as planned, they'll be here looking for them, thought Matthew.

"Okay, I will send Cindy over right away," said H.G.

Cindy took the van to Matthew's house. She knew that what she was doing wasn't right. She knew if H.G. found out she had called Gracie and switched the lockets that morning when she went to see Matthew, she was going to be the one in trouble. Matthew had given Cindy the locket to give back to Gracie. Matthew had taken the fake one. They weren't going to let Peter know about the plan. Peter was deathly afraid of his father. He had told H.G. that Matthew would have the real locket. He had told him he'd gotten rid of the fake one. H.G. didn't know that Peter had given Cindy the fake locket. When she went to see Matthew that morning, she had switched the lockets. H.G. didn't know that Matthew had given Katie and Penny a paralyzing drug that would make it seem as if they were dead. He didn't let Peter know about that bit of information either.

Cindy got to Matthew's house and parked the van as close to the house as she could. They all helped carry Penny and Katie to the back of the van for H.G.'s approval. They drove to the guesthouse. Cindy drove in front with the van, Matthew followed her in his SUV, and Peter was behind him. Matthew parked his SUV right behind the van. Peter pulled his car into the garage. H.G. came out and looked at the girls' bodies.

"Well, Matt, you did your father proud. Now, why don't you come join us?"

"You know why I did what I did. I want to see Mom." To keep up with the plan, Matthew had had to tell everyone his mom was dead.

"Don't worry; you will in time."

"No, we had a deal. I kept my end of the bargain up. You need to show me my mother."

"Come on in, and get comfortable. You're not finished yet."

"What do you mean? You got what you wanted. The girls who could hurt you most are gone. As soon as you show me my mother, you'll have your locket."

"Matt, I said come inside. We can make the switch."

Matthew gave him an angry look. "H.G., I said you will get what you want when you show me my mother."

Peter came walking around the corner. "What is going on here? Dad, what are you saying?"

"Peter, your job is finished here. Now, go inside!"

Peter shook his head. "No, I want to know what is going on. You told me they were going to kill you if I didn't help Matt get the locket. It sounds to me like you have a different story than the one you told me."

"Peter, this is none of your business. This is between me and your brother."

"My girlfriend is dead in the back of the van, and you're telling me it's none of my business?"

"Come on, Peter. She was nothing but a piece of trash you took out."

Peter stormed toward H.G., slammed right into his father, and knocked him over. "I should have never listened to you. I wish I would have never helped you!"

Just then, the watch started spinning, and the hourglass flipped upside down.

Peter found himself back at Matthew's house. Katie, Penny, and Matthew were all sitting on the couch. "Well, that didn't go as planned. Wait—how did we get back here?" Peter looked at Penny and hugged her.

"I'm not so sure I can be with you, Peter. By all rights, you thought I was dead. You were willing to kill me for your father," Penny said with tears rolling down her face.

"I'm sorry to have to do this to you, but we are running out of time. You two are going to have to talk about this later." Matthew went to the kitchen to get the iced tea. When he came back, he said, "Peter, you can't give us away. Now you know what is going on. Dad has my mother in that house. I need you to help."

"Don't worry, Matt. I'm behind you one hundred percent. Penny, now that I know you're not out to kill my dad, I'm behind you too."

Katie looked at them. "Once we get through tonight, we all have a lot to talk about."

CHAPTER 31

Redo

"Well, Peter, now that you know what's going on, are you with us?" Matthew asked.

"Of course, I'm with you."

Matthew looked at Peter. "We have to let Dad think things are going as planned. Although there is one thing, I left out that I can't share with you until I know Mom is safe. Peter, you must follow my directions. To the word!"

"Matt, you don't have to tell me twice. I'll know when it's time."

"Penny, Katie, are you two ready? You know you'll have to drink that nasty tea again. It's the only way he will think you're dead."

Katie looked at Matthew and gave him a thumbs-up. She and Penny drank the tea.

"Okay, Peter, you can call Dad. They're out."

Peter called his father. "Tell Cindy to bring down the van. It's done."

Cindy got to the house, and they all put Penny and Katie in the back of the van. They returned to the guesthouse, and H.G. and his guests came out to look at the bodies.

"Well done, Matt. Now, come inside, and let's finish what we started."

Matthew followed his father into the guesthouse. Peter was right behind him. They put on their black robes and gathered around the pentagram in the middle of the room. Each member took his place by a point of the star.

"Gentlemen, we are gathered here tonight to call upon the powers of the locket. We each have a person in our lives who has caused us grave danger. I ask you now to enter the circle a picture of the person you'd like to remove from your life. Pastor Joe, you go first."

Pastor Joe threw a picture of Brody's mom into the center of the circle.

"Pete, you're next."

Pete threw a picture of Paula's grandmother into the center of the circle.

"Matt, it's your turn."

Matthew threw a picture of Katie into the circle.

"Peter, it's your turn."

Peter threw a picture of Penny into the circle.

"Last but not least, it's my turn to go." H.G. threw a picture of Kimberly into the circle. He knew if he got rid of Kimberly, he could be with Melinda. H.G. turned to Matthew. "Son, did you bring the locket?"

"Yes, sir." Matthew handed the locket to his father.

"We ask you, by the powers of the locket, to hold these women inside until we are ready to release them."

Gracie and Naomi came from out of the corner. The room started to fill with smoke. Naomi was pointing a steam machine toward the men. Gracie yelled, "Now!"

Matthew and Peter jumped back away from the pentagram. Gracie recited the following words: "Come into the locket, H.G., Joe, and Pete, where you will reside until you are called back from the other side."

The three men turned to dust and swirled inside the locket.

Gracie looked at Naomi. "It's done. Let's go get the girls. Matt, your mother is in the kitchen at the big house with Cindy."

"Thank you, Gracie."

Peter looked at Matthew. "Hey, Matt, did you think you were keeping those two a secret from me? Is that what you couldn't tell me? Because I saw them in the back of your SUV. So, if that is what it was, nice try, Brother."

Matthew looked at Peter. "Now the real work begins." Matthew and Peter went out to meet the girls.

Penny hugged Peter. "Thank you for saving us!"

Katie walked up to the house with Matthew right beside her. She started asking Matthew all kinds of questions. "How did you get Nana and Gracie to come to the guesthouse? How did you know when to leave the pentagram? When did you, Gracie, and Nana meet to talk about all of this?"

"Whoa, slow down. We can talk about all this tomorrow. Tonight, I would like you to meet my mother."

"Wait—what if she doesn't like me?" Katie said.

"She will love you!"

Katie looked at Matthew and stopped him from going inside. "I need to ask you a question. How did you know the watch would work to get us to go back in time?"

Matthew looked over at Peter. "I was counting on my brother to speak from his heart. When he learned that Dad was keeping my mom from me, he felt like Dad had betrayed him. That's when the watch works the best. Am I right?"

"You're right. But you put a lot of faith in Peter tonight."

"I'm just glad he's more like his mom than our dad," Matthew said. "Now, can we go meet my mom? I'll answer more questions later."

CHAPTER 32

The Questioning

Morning came with a majestic sunrise. Katie was feeling good about life. Graduation was a week away. She and Matthew were going to go camping on the beach after graduation. She was taking time off from the BSU. Peter and Penny were going to join them. It had been a while since the locket incident.

Kimberly was back at home, answering a lot of questions about H.G.'s whereabouts. She told everyone that H.G. had left town, and she wasn't sure when he'd be back. She was happy to be out of rehab and back home with her children. She was also happy that H.G. wasn't around.

Life seemed to be going great for everyone.

It came to a screeching halt when Detective Knapp came knocking on their door. Cindy answered.

"Hey, Cindy, any news from H.G.?" asked Jack.

"Not that I'm aware of."

"Is Mrs. Sampson in?"

"Yes, I will tell her you're here to see her."

Kimberly came out of H.G.'s office. "Detective Knapp, what a nice surprise. What can I help you with today?"

Jack looked right into Kimberly's eyes. "Have you heard anything from H.G.?"

"No, I wish I could give you something different, Detective. But as I stated before, he was gone before I came back from rehab."

"I was told by an unnamed source that H.G., Pastor Joe Horton, and Pete DeSoto were all here the night they disappeared. Can you confirm that for me?" Jack asked.

"I would love to, Detective; however, as I have told you and the others who have come calling for my husband, I was away when he apparently took off. Peter is upset that he isn't around. My son graduates next week. His father is MIA."

"What is that supposed to mean?"

"Missing in action."

"I know what MIA stands for, but I don't get the correlation between your husband not being here and him being MIA. Unless you know something, I don't."

"Detective, I'm really getting tired of repeating myself. I don't know where H.G. is or when he will be back. I was away when he took off. Now, if you don't have anything else to tell me or question me about, you may leave."

"Thank you for your time, Mrs. Sampson. If you hear from H.G., you'll let us know?"

"Of course, I will, Detective. Now, good day." Kimberly shut the door after Jack left. She needed to get the group together. It was getting harder to answer the questions.

CHAPTER 33

The Meeting

Kimberly called Gracie. She needed them all to get together that night to figure out what they were going to do with H.G. and the other men they'd put inside the locket. She thought they should take everything to Detective Knapp. Katie had information on Pastor Joe and knew about Pete DeSoto. She said that Jimmy Benson, Brody's brother, would testify against Pastor Joe. They just needed to get the dirt on Pete. Maybe they could bring him out and set him up.

As far as H.G. coming out of the locket, Kimberly was taking care of his business and didn't need him around, although Detective Knapp had been looking for him. Gracie told Kimberly they would all be at her house at seven o'clock. That way, everyone would be home from school or work, and they wouldn't have anyone around to disrupt them, meaning there wouldn't be any stragglers.

It was close to seven o'clock. Naomi, Katie, Matthew, Peter, and Penny were waiting for Gracie to arrive. Kimberly asked Cindy to make iced tea for everyone. She also asked Cindy to join them. Edith opened the front door when Gracie rang the doorbell. Gracie entered the living room, where everyone was sitting around talking.

"Did any of you watch the news at six o'clock?" Gracie asked. "They had H.G., Pastor Joe, and Pete DeSoto's pictures plastered all over the news, asking anyone who had seen any of them to contact the local sheriff's office."

Everyone shook his or her head. Cindy walked in with Kimberly behind her.

"Would anyone like some iced tea?" Cindy asked.

Katie and Penny both shook their heads. Naomi and Gracie each took a glass, as did Matthew and Peter.

Naomi said, "Gracie and I have been discussing our little dilemma. What if we were to bring them out one at a time and make them pay for their crimes? We can tell them if they don't go to the police and confess, they will go back into the locket."

"Naomi, that sounds like a fantastic idea in theory, but do you really think they will hold up their end of the bargain?" Matthew said.

"Matt, do you have any other suggestions?" Naomi looked at him and raised her eyebrows.

"I think we should take Jimmy to the police station—and anyone else we can find who is willing to talk about what Pastor Joe did to him. Get the police involved before we let them out. Also, we know by the picture that Pete DeSoto threw into the pentagram that he wants to get rid of Paula's grandmother. We need to find out what that is all about. What does she have over him? Then there is Dad. Well, we can keep him in there for a while before we need to bring him back. Katie, can you get with Jimmy tomorrow and ask him to meet you at the police station? Maybe Gracie or Naomi could visit Paula's grandmother and get some answers from her."

Peter stood up and asked what he and Penny should do.

"You both have a week of school left," Matthew said. "Why don't you put all your energies into getting to school so you can graduate, Peter? And, Penny, I know junior year isn't easy. You must need to take some tests."

"You know, Matt, you're probably right. This last week of senior year is crazy. There is so much to do before I walk down that aisle and get my diploma," Peter said sarcastically.

"Just get to school, Peter."

Penny patted Peter on the knee and said they would. Matthew looked at the group and asked them all to meet back there at seven o'clock tomorrow night. They all agreed and said good night.

Kimberly pulled Matthew to the side. "Can I have a word with you?"

"Sure, let me say good night to Katie."

Matthew walked out, kissed Katie good night, and said goodbye to Nana. They took off down the road. Kimberly looked at Matt and asked him where they were holding H.G. and the other men.

"Kimberly, you're better off not knowing. That way, when the cops come asking questions, you don't have to lie about their whereabouts."

Kimberly nodded, agreeing with Matthew. "How is your mother doing?"

"She's good. She went back to Chicago. My grandparents

are due back from Australia, and she wanted to be home to greet them."

"I'm glad to hear she is okay. Matt, I'm really sorry about your father."

"You don't have to apologize for anything, Kimberly. He made his choices in life. Now, if we are finished, I would like to go home, get something to eat, and relax. I will see you tomorrow."

"Okay. Goodnight Matt."

"Good night."

CHAPTER 34

~

Clint

Katie called the sheriff's department to see if she could meet with Detective Knapp that afternoon.

"Detective Knapp, Pennsylvania Sheriff's Department. What can I help you with?"

"Hi, Detective. It's Katie O'Reilly. I was wondering if I could come in this afternoon to talk to you."

"Katie, what is this in reference to?"

"I'd like to talk to you about Pastor Joe. I'm bringing in a young man who has some serious accusations against Pastor Joe. I would like you to hear him out."

"You know he is missing, right?"

"I do, but I would still like to talk to you about him."

"Sure, Katie, what time?"

"Around four o'clock."

"I will see you when you get here."

Katie called Jimmy to let him know what time the

appointment was. He asked her to pick him up. He would have another kid with him.

"Where do you want me to pick you up?" Katie asked.

"Can you meet us at the school, outside where the bus picks up the kids?" Jimmy asked.

"I will be there at three forty-five."

Jimmy thanked Katie for all she was trying to do.

Katie was at the school at 3:10, waiting for Jimmy and his friend. She spotted him in her rear-view mirror. She honked her horn, waving her hand out the window. He walked up to the car with a kid named Clint Turnball. They knocked on the window on the opposite side of the car. The door was locked, and they were trying to get in. Jimmy started introducing Clint to Katie, when Clint took off running. Jimmy ran after him, caught his shirttail, and put him on the ground.

"Why are you running, Clint?"

Clint looked at Jimmy with tears coming down his face. "I don't want Pastor Joe to find out that I snitched on him. If he finds out, there's no telling what he will do to my mother or my little sister. He also said he was going to take away the money he's been giving my mother."

"Clint, I told you Katie will help you. She said they have government programs that help people who can't pay their bills. Plus, you're not only helping yourself; you're helping all the other boys this monster has molested. You're also helping Brody. If we don't stop him, you know there will be more. You have proof. I don't have that. I just have hearsay. Come on, Clint. Let's go meet Katie."

They walked to the car together. Katie rolled her window down, and Clint introduced himself.

"Nice to meet you, Clint. You boys ready to do this? Don't worry. If you need anything, I will be right with you," Katie said.

"Yeah, we're ready." Jimmy got into the front seat.

Clint hopped in the back.

"Guys, I know this can't be easy for you. If you want, I will be in the interview room with you."

Jimmy and Clint both thanked Katie.

They arrived at the sheriff's station five minutes early.

"Detective Knapp said he would meet us in the lobby," Katie said.

They all walked inside together. The lobby was a small room with glass separating the guard on duty from the outside room. On the wall was a telephone. Above the telephone was a sign: "Please pick up the phone for instructions." Katie picked up the phone, and the guard answered it.

"State the reason why you're here."

"We have an appointment with Detective Knapp."

"Take a seat. I will let him know you're here."

Katie, Clint, and Jimmy sat in the lounge chairs, waiting for the detective. About ten minutes went by before the door opened.

"Katie O'Reilly?"

"Here, sir," Katie said.

"Follow me into my office," Detective Knapp said.

The boys stood up and followed Katie.

"All right, why don't you tell me the reason why you are here today?"

Katie spoke up first. "Detective, these two boys would like to bring criminal charges against Pastor Joe Horton for molestation."

Jack looked up from his paper and raised his eyebrows. "You do realize the man is missing? You also need to realize these are some serious accusations. Do you have any proof?"

Clint reached inside his backpack. "Would a pair of my jeans with the pastor's semen on them be good enough proof?"

Jack picked up the phone. "Johnny, can you come to my office with a big plastic bag to pick up some evidence?"

Johnny came into Jack's office with rubber gloves on and a plastic bag.

"Thanks, Johnny."

"Sure thing, Jack. I'll have the lab run the DNA ASAP." Johnny left the room.

Jack turned to Katie. "What do you have to do with any of this, Ms. O'Reilly?"

"Well, one of my clients at the BSU who recently took his life was molested by Pastor Joe. Can I bring my testimony to the table?"

"Unfortunately, that would be inadmissible. When was all this supposed to have taken place?"

Jimmy spoke first. "He tried to molest me a few years ago. It was my brother who killed himself."

"I'm sorry for your loss. Do you have any proof?" Jack asked.

"No, sir, not other than my testimony."

"What about you, young man?"

Clint asked if he could speak to him alone.

"Tell you what. There is a TV room down the hall from my office on the right. You two can wait in there. I will talk to Mr. Turnball, and then I will get your statement, Mr. Benson."

Katie and Jimmy left the room. Katie looked at Jimmy. "Are you nervous, Jimmy?"

"Nah, I just hope Clint has enough on Pastor Joe to put him away for a very long time."

"Yeah, me too."

They sat in the lounge chairs with the news on the TV behind them. Suddenly, they saw H.G. Sampson, Joe Horton, and Pete DeSoto's faces on the news. "If anyone has seen any of these men, please contact the sheriff's department."

Katie looked at the floor. It was tiled with a pattern of diamonds inside squares. She started tracing them with her eyes. They waited awhile before Clint came into the TV room.

"Jimmy, the detective wants to hear what you have to say."

Jimmy left, and Clint sat down. "I just want to thank you, Katie. For some reason, I feel better."

"You're very welcome, Clint."

Another fifteen minutes went by before Jimmy came into the TV room.

"Detective Knapp said he would be in touch. We can go."

They all walked out of the sheriff's department and got into Katie's car.

"Katie, can I ask you to drop me off at Jimmy's house? I don't want my mother finding anything out just yet," Clint said.

"Sure, Clint."

She dropped the boys off at Jimmy's house, and they all said their goodbyes. She drove away, feeling better about the situation. She knew the boys both felt better after what they had just done. She drove home to take a shower before she had to meet up with the group. She thought she would let them know it was time to get Pastor Joe out of the locket. *That man won't know what hit him. Hopefully they will get the DNA back from the jeans, and they can convict the bastard.*

CHAPTER 35

Award Ceremony

Katie and Nana headed for Kimberly's house. It was almost seven thirty in the evening. They had gotten a late start because Katie was at the sheriff's department until six o'clock with the boys. By the time she'd gotten home, eaten dinner, and taken a shower, it was later than she'd thought. They parked outside the Sampson house, and Matthew was at the front door to greet them.

Katie gave Matthew a quick kiss on the cheek, and Nana and Katie followed Matthew inside. Kimberly and Gracie were waiting in the living room. Penny and Peter hadn't joined the group yet. Katie noticed first.

"Where are Peter and Penny?"

Kimberly looked at Katie, a little shocked. "They had an awards ceremony to go to. He took Penny as a guest."

"Oh crap, that's tonight!" Katie said.

"Katie, why don't you go? We can do this another night, or we can do this later this evening," said Matthew.

"No, I have a lot of information for the group."

Matthew looked at Katie. "Come on, Katie. This is your last week of school. You should be there."

"Matt, you know how important this is to me. I will give you all the rundown of what happened earlier, and then I will think about it."

She told them about Jimmy. Then she told them about Clint and his proof of the molestation. She told them Detective Knapp was taking on the investigation and was going to help them put that rat bastard behind bars. "I think it's time for Pastor Joe to come out of the locket and face the consequences," Katie said.

Naomi then said, "Katie, you have time to make it to the school for the awards ceremony. You should leave now. We can do this later. One more day won't hurt."

"Matt, I didn't get you a ticket."

"Don't worry about me. You need to have this experience."

Katie looked at the group. "Seeing as you are all willing to get rid of me, I think I will go." She giggled. "But I will be back tonight." Before she left, she gave Nana a kiss on the cheek and then gave Matthew a kiss. "Don't start without me."

Katie got into her car and headed for the school. She looked down at her phone. She had six messages, all from Jamie. The phone pinged again. She looked at it quickly.

When she looked back up, a car was headed right for her. She swerved into a ditch.

The next thing she knew, everything went black.

CHAPTER 36

The Accident

Penny and Peter got back to the house. Peter had won Guy Most Improved from Freshman Year. It was all in fun.

Penny looked around the group. "Where is Katie?"

Matthew looked up. "What do you mean? Katie went to the awards ceremony."

"We didn't see her. She won an academic award. She wasn't there to receive it," Peter said.

Naomi spoke up. "I'm going to call her friend Jamie. If anyone knows where Katie is, it would be Jamie."

Jamie answered on the first ring.

"Jamie, this is Katie's nana. Have you seen Katie tonight?"

"No, I just figured she was with Matt. I tried calling her and texting her. Her phone went dead around eight o'clock," Jamie said.

"Well, Matt is here with me. I'm going to give the hospitals a call."

"Please let me know what you find out."

"I will, Jamie. Talk to you later."

Naomi started calling the local hospitals. No one had seen Katie, and no one with her description had been brought in that night. "Where could she be?"

"I'm going to get in the car and start looking for her." Matthew grabbed his coat.

Naomi walked out with him. "Do you mind if I come along?"

"Not at all."

Penny and Peter got in their car and went looking for her. They traced the roads to the school.

Matthew and Naomi got to Naomi's house, but Katie's car wasn't in the driveway.

"Matt, can you drop me off? If someone finds her, they'll probably call the house. I will call you if I hear anything."

Matthew drove around looking for signs of Katie. He took the road that Katie would have gone on to get to the school. Then he spotted her car. It was in the ditch. There were no skid marks alongside the road to suggest she had any idea whatever was going to hit her car, that she was prepared for it He dialed 911 with his cell phone.

The operator came on. "This is 911. What's your emergency?"

"My girlfriend's car is lying in a ditch off Route 220, just around the corner from the gas station."

"Is she hurt?"

"I don't know. I just came upon the accident. Her car is upside down, though."

Matthew slid down into the ditch, hoping to find Katie

alive. She was hanging upside down. The seat belt was the only thing holding her in. The car was leaking fluid. He wasn't sure where it was coming from. He went back to his vehicle to grab his knife. The operator was asking him all kinds of questions, but he wasn't listening at that point. He needed to get Katie out and away from the car. He opened his glove compartment and took his knife out. Then he slid back down into the ditch.

"Katie, can you hear me?" Matthew yelled.

She was still alive. He tried to cut the seat belt and hold her at the same time so she wouldn't fall. Matthew was desperate to get her away from the car's leaking fluid. An ambulance finally arrived, and EMTs pushed Matthew out of the way.

"Sir, can you tell us what happened?" one asked.

"No, I just spotted her car. I'm not sure what went on or how she landed in the ditch."

"Thank you, sir. Now, step away from the vehicle, please."

A fire truck arrived and shut down the area around the accident. The medical team worked hard, trying to release Katie from the seat belt. Finally, she was freed and eased out of the car. The team put her on a stretcher and loaded her in the ambulance. Katie was calling for Matthew, who reassured her before they took her away, "I will follow behind in my car."

Matthew called Katie's nana, told her about the accident, and said to meet him at Saint Joseph's Hospital.

Katie was being wheeled into the hospital when her nana arrived. Matthew was inside, in the waiting area.

"Matt, what happened?"

"I'm not sure. I went looking for her and spotted her car flipped upside down in a ditch. I don't know anything other than that. I dialed 911, and they came and pulled her out. Now you know as much as I do."

The doctor came out into the waiting room. "Is there someone here for Ms. O'Reilly?"

"I am her grandmother."

"She would like to see you."

Nana followed the doctor into her room. "Katie, sweetheart, what happened?"

"Nana, the watch!" She could barely speak.

"What did you say, sweetie?"

Katie tried opening her eyes. "The watch." She fell back into a deep sleep.

The machines monitoring Katie's vitals started going off. There were all kinds of hoses attached to her body. Just then, a bunch of nurses and doctors came rushing into the room.

"Mrs. O'Reilly, we're going to have to ask you to step out," the doctor said.

Naomi looked at Katie and said, "I wish this didn't happen. I wish I could have been with you."

Papa's watch started spinning out of control.

Katie woke up in the hospital.

Nana looked at her. "Oh, sweetie, I didn't think you were ever going to come back."

"Where am I, Nana?"

"Sweetheart, you're in the hospital. You have been here for months. You got into a bad car accident while coming home from school one night."

"Wait—what are you saying, Nana? What about Matthew, Peter, Penny, Gracie, and Kimberly?"

"Sweetheart, I don't know what you're talking about. The

doctors said you hit your head hard. They didn't think you were going to come out of the coma. I'm so happy to see you. I'm so glad you're alive. Jamie has been here every day, talking to you. I need to call her to let her know you're awake. She was praying you would wake up before graduation."

"What's the date today?"

"May 17. You have a few days before graduation. I have talked to all your teachers. They said you have enough credits to be able to graduate with your class. That is, if you feel up to it."

"So, Nana, you're telling me I have been in a coma for the last several months? Everything I have been through was just a dream?"

"Katie, I'm not quite following you, sweetie. I'm not sure what you think you've been through, but you have been in a coma for several months."

"I can't believe it. Everything was so real."

"The doctors are saying you could be out by the end of the week. Graduation is on Monday; you can at least attend graduation."

Katie wasn't sure of anything. Everything that had happened in the last several months had been just a dream? She couldn't wrap her head around it. Jamie came into her room.

"Oh, Katie, thank God you're awake. I've missed you!"

"Jamie, how long have I been here?"

Jamie gave her an odd look. "Months, Katie. But guess what? We are graduating on Monday!"

Nana told Jamie she had to keep the visit to a minimum.

"Katie, once you get sprung from here, we will have to do something together. Especially after school is over."

"Sounds good, Jamie."

Nana looked at Jamie and told her Katie had had enough for one day. Jamie hugged her and said goodbye.

Katie was confused. She couldn't believe what Nana had said about everything being a dream. She had to believe Matthew was real. She loved him. "Nana, I'm really tired. Can we talk later?"

CHAPTER 37

Is She Dreaming?

Katie couldn't remember much of anything. The only thing she knew was that Matthew existed. She couldn't possibly forget him. *Maybe Nana was right, and it was all just a dream.*

Dr. Brannish came into the room and asked if she was ready to go home. "Your grandmother will pick you up later today. Katie, do me a favor. Wear a helmet from now on."

She giggled and nodded.

Nana arrived at the hospital at noon. She and Dr. Brannish talked in the corner for some time before they brought a wheelchair over to her bed.

Nana said, "Dr. Brannish is going to let you attend graduation. He said you will be able to pick up your diploma, but you'll have to come home and rest after the ceremony. I have already spoken to Jamie about it. She is going to come home with you for a while."

Katie shook her head. "I don't want her to miss out on any of the parties. She doesn't need to be with me."

"You will have to talk to Jamie about that."

Dr. Brannish told her, "Hop on the express chair leaving this station."

Katie thought, *this feels a little like déjà vu.* An orderly wheeled her out to Nana's car, which was already waiting for her when she got to the exit.

"Are you ready to go home?" Nana asked.

"Yes, I am. I feel pretty good. Although I am having trouble with my memory. I see bits and pieces of what may have taken place in the last several months, but I can't remember if it's real or if it's just a dream."

"The doctor said you are going to slowly get your memory back. He said if you remember too much too soon, he might have to put you into a medically induced coma. Too many memories at once might put you back where you just came from. He wants you to take it easy."

They drove home in silence.

Monday morning came, and Katie got a phone call from Jamie.

"O'Reilly, you ready to begin the rest of your life? Once we get our diplomas, we are starting a new chapter. I'm so happy you are going to be at graduation."

"Jamie, I want you to go out tonight to the graduation parties. You don't have to babysit me."

"Katie, you have been my best friend for like forever. I'm going to be with you after one of the most important times in our lives."

"Okay, Jamie, I see there is no point in arguing with you.

I will see you tonight." Katie hung the phone up, and Nana walked into her room. She had a gift in her hand.

"Your papa wanted me to make sure you got this before graduation."

Katie opened the present. It was a locket—a unique-looking one. She swore she had seen it before. "Thank you, Nana. This means a lot to me. I feel as though Papa is with me." Katie put the locket on.

Nana left the room.

Katie felt something odd. It was as if the locket were trying to tell her something. It felt weird. She ignored the feeling and went downstairs for breakfast.

Later, Katie was getting ready for graduation. Nana had picked her dress up from the store. She was excited and nervous to be getting her diploma that night. Finally, after thirteen years of school, she was going to be able to move on with the next chapter of her life.

She came down and headed for the kitchen, where Nana was fixing some snack platters for later. "Katie, you look absolutely beautiful."

"Thank you, Nana."

"I'm just going to cover these platters, and then I will be ready," Nana said. "Why don't you get yourself in the car?"

Katie walked to the car and got inside. She was waiting on her grandmother, when she saw an SUV drive by. She wasn't sure of the significance, but she knew she had seen that vehicle before.

They arrived at the school, and everyone who was graduating lined up onstage.

While sitting through the speeches, Katie kept getting

flashbacks. She didn't know if they were real or part of her dream. Then she heard her name being called: "Katlyn Rae O'Reilly." That was her cue to go pick up her diploma. She walked toward the principal.

"Congratulations, Katie."

"Thank you, Mr. Wilson." They shook hands.

As Katie walked away, she looked up. "Matthew!"

ABOUT THE AUTHOR

MICHELE KNECHT has lived in Florida, California, Australia, Maine, and Pennsylvania. She currently resides in northeastern Pennsylvania with her husband, daughter, and dogs. When she is not writing, she can be found visiting her other daughter and son-in-law in upstate New York. This is her first book.

Printed in the United States
By Bookmasters